Joy

In

The

Morning

By

TAMMY L. ARCHIBALD

ISBN: 1-4107-7128-8 (e-book)
ISBN: 1-4107-7129-6 (Paperback)

This book is printed on acid free paper.

1stBooks – rev. 09/26/03

PREFACE

When I was born stretching through the tightness of my Mother's womb, I'm here at last I thought, as I took my first breath. So, this is life. I opened my eyes for the first time expecting to see the face of the person whom I would come to know as my Mother. I would call her mama, ma, or even mommy. Then, I saw her. She was beautiful and she was mine. You did well, I thought. You brought me into this world. I was so elated. But, the feeling did not last for long. Suddenly I felt another presence engulfing me, overcoming my feelings of happiness and love. This presence revealed to me, pain and sorrow. "Who are you," I asked? "I am your storm," it said. "I am death and I want you." I looked up into my Mother's face. Why did you bring me into this world I thought, as I cried my first cry.

In this world, you shall have tribulation: ***BUT*** be of good cheer Jesus has overcome the world.

WEEPING MAY ENDURE FOR A NIGHT BUT JOY COMES IN THE MORNING

ACKNOWLEDGEMENTS

This book is gratefully dedicated to my grandmother, Evangelist Mattie Barnes, my mother, Rev. Dr. Mamie L. Archibald, my brothers, Alphonso and Michael, and my sisters, Gwen and Mattie Renee. I appreciate all of your love and support. Thanks to my basketball players, Dominique and little Malik. To Charity, you are love. Thanks to my wonderful and beautiful young lady, Jasmine Archibald. Special thanks to Linda for your encouragement, support, and friendship.

In loving memory of Alphonso Archibald Sr.

SISTERS

Whap! Whap!

"Mama don't."

Whap! Whap!

The sound of the belt was piercingly loud.

Whap! Whap!

Joy could hear her sister Verna cry out from their bedroom for their mama to stop.

"You little nothing," Mama yelled.

Whap! Joy could not take it anymore. All she could hear was the sound of the belt hitting her sister's flesh. Whap! Whap! Whap!

"No more," Joy screamed.

She burst through the bedroom door.

"Stop Mama, that's enough!"

Verna was laid out on the bed naked. Whenever their mama got angry, she would tell them to take their clothes off. That meant they had a whipping coming.

"Mama please," Joy begged. "Don't hit her no more."

Mama raised the belt again and again.

Whap! Whap!

The whelps on Verna's back began to bleed. Verna lay on the bed refusing to cry.

"Please Verna cry," Joy screamed.

"You know if you don't cry she ain't going to stop."

Verna refused to cry. She just laid there biting her lips as each blow cut through her delicate skin. Mama continued on.

"If you talk back to me again, this whipping ain't gonna mean nothing compared to the one you gonna get." "Now get out of my house and don't come back until tomorrow, because if I see you before then, I'm gonna whip your black butt some more."

"But Mama," Verna cried. "I don't have anywhere to go. Please mama it is so cold out there."

Whap! Whap!

The belt came down again and again.

"I'm going mama," Verna cried. "I ain't never coming back again. You hear me mama, never!"

"You will be back," Mama said.

Joy could see that Verna meant it this time. Joy began to cry.

"Don't go Verna. Please don't leave me alone with Mama."

"You shut your mouth Joy," Mama snapped. "Your butt will be next."

Joy watched as Verna began to grab a few things.

"You can just leave that stuff right here," Mama said. "I bought all that stuff. You ain't taking nothing with you." Joy watched as Verna walked out the door. Somehow she knew that her sister would never come back.

Mama was a tall, big boned woman with a copper tan complexion. She had what some black people called good hair. She wore it short and naturally curly. Mama never talked about her Father, but it was rumored that Mama's Mother had been raped by three white men and one of the three was her Father. Mama's Mother

3

died when Mama was six years old. It was never really clear how she died. Some people said she died of grief. She never could deal with how dirty she felt. She could never touch the baby which was a constant reminder of what had happened. Mama was raised by her Grandmother until she died from a heart attack when Mama was twelve. She was then raised by a Great Aunt until she was put out at the age of sixteen. Mama met Verna and Joy's Father at the age of 17. He was ten years older than Mama. They married six months later when Mama became pregnant with her first child, Verna. Verna was named after her Father, Vernon. Two years later, their second child Joy was born. He named her because she was his bundle of joy. Six months later Verna and Joy's Father was shot dead during an armed robbery. Witnesses reported that he had refused to give up his wallet and was shot at point blank range by a junkie. He only had five dollars in his wallet. Mama remarried and had two other children. Her husband's name was Buddell. But he insisted that Joy and Verna call him Stepdaddy. He was quick to remind them, "I ain't yo Daddy." Their first child was Buddell Jr. Junior was 12 years old. Junior looked like Mama with her complexion and curly hair. Janet better known as Precious was the baby of the family. She was eight and could do no wrong. Precious was also copper tan with long black silky hair. She had grey eyes. Precious was Mama's pride and joy. She was a straight A student. She skipped a grade and was in honor classes. Mama only bought the best for Precious. Verna and Joy had to wear hand me down and cheap clothing. Mama said it was because Precious was going to make something out of herself and needed nice things to wear. One day Verna said she was going to make something out of herself too. Mama reached over and slapped Verna in the mouth. Stepdaddy laughed. Joy cried.

Verna and Joy took after their father. They were both tall for their ages, 17 and 15. They were both dark brown. Verna wore a short afro. Joy's hair was shoulder length. Verna would press it for her every Tuesday. They both had large almond shaped eyes. Their friends said this was their best feature.

As Joy lay in her bed, all she could think about was Verna was gone. She felt so alone.

"Oh Verna please come back. Don't leave me alone."

Joy dozed off. She awoke to a tap on the window.

"Open up, it's me," Verna said through the open window.

Joy quickly opened the window.

"Verna you came back."

"I'm not back," Verna said. "I came to get my stuff. Forget Mama. I'm taking all my stuff." Joy watched as Verna packed some things in a small back pack. She watched Verna grab a pocket sized Bible off the dresser. This was the only thing they had that belonged to their deceased Father. "Take me with you Verna. Please don't leave me."

"I can't take you with me. Not right now. I promise you as soon as I get myself together; I will come back for you, Joy."

"Verna, please stay longer. We can go together."

"No," Verna said. "Listen to me. This is something I have to do. I am 17 and you are only 15. Stay here and stay in school. I promise I will help you find a way out as soon as I can. Mama was never as hard on you as she is on me. You can make it here a little longer."

Joy was upset. "Where are you going?"

"I am going to stay with my friend Sue Kinley. I promise I will get in touch with you. Do not do anything until you hear from me, o.k.?"

"O.k.," Joy replied. The tears were falling down her face.

As Verna stepped toward the window to leave, she turned back to Joy. It hurt her to leave Joy.

"Please don't cry. Remember when we were little and Mama took us to church. Remember how the Preacher said something about crying for a night but in the morning joy comes. Well, you are my Joy in the morning and don't you ever forget it." Verna reached in the back pack and took out a pen. She took the Bible and wrote in it. She handed the Bible to Joy.

"You keep this."

Joy's hand began to tremble. "No, Verna this means so much to you."

"Yes it does. I want you to keep it."

Joy watched as Verna walked away into the dark night. She could feel the cold brisk air against her tears. Joy opened the Bible. In big bold letters she read, YOU ARE MY JOY IN THE

MORNING. The next morning Joy learned that last night was one of the coldest nights of the year.

The next morning Mama was banging dishes everywhere. Joy could tell she was in a nasty mood. Precious, Junior, and Stepdaddy were sitting at the table eating breakfast.

"Well, Well, Well," Stepdaddy said looking at Joy. "Sit down and eat some breakfast."

"I am not hungry," Joy said.

Stepdaddy's eyes roamed up and down Joy's thin body. Joy's body was beginning to develop. For the past few months, Joy had noticed him looking at her a lot. She tried to avoid Stepdaddy whenever she could. "I am not hungry," Joy said.

Stepdaddy reached into his pocket and pulled out some candy. "Daddy has some candy for all his babies." He gave Junior and Precious each a bag of candy.

"Don't you want your candy Joy?"

"No sir."

Stepdaddy looked hard at Joy.

"You an ungrateful one ain't ya. You are getting just like your
sorry sister. Get over here and let Stepdaddy give you some
candy."

Joy snapped.

"Don't you talk about my sister. She is all I got. You ain't my
daddy. My daddy is dead."

Joy felt a stinging pain on her head. Mama had hit her with the
wet dish cloth.

"He is the only daddy you got," Mama snapped. "I don't want to
hear you say that again. Now go over there and tell him you are
sorry." Joy just stood there. She felt another wet blow to her
head. "Get your butt over there right now," Mama screamed.
Junior picked up his school books and walked out the front door.
Precious sat at the table with her head down. Joy walked up to
Stepdaddy. He grabbed Joy and pulled her close to him. Joy
could feel a throbbing bulge between Stepdaddy's legs. She tried
to pull back, but he continued to hold her between his legs.

"Say it," Mama yelled.

"I'm Sorry," Joy whispered.

"Say I'm sorry, daddy." Stepdaddy emphasized.

Joy paused. Stepdaddy pulled her closer. Tears of despair began

to fall down her face.

"I'm sorry Daddy."

"That's a lot better he said. Stepdaddy let Joy go. Joy ran to her

room in tears.

"Oh Verna, please hurry back for me."

Joy grabbed her school books and hurried out the door.

She almost tripped over something. She looked down and saw the

bag of candy that Stepdaddy had given Junior beside the trash

can. As she walked to school thoughts of hatred of Stepdaddy

filled her mind.

"I hate Stepdaddy, I hate Stepdaddy, I hate Stepdaddy. He is not

my daddy."

Stepdaddy was a big man. He weighed almost three hundred

pounds of pure fat. He was light brown and had beady eyes. Joy

did not know why Mama loved him so much. As Joy walked to

school, a feeling of dread overcame her. She needed Verna. She

turned around and ran towards the bottom. The bottom was just that. It was the worst section of the projects where pimps, prostitutes, and drug addicts hung out. Joy had never gone there alone before but she knew she had to go there because that is where Verna's friend Sue Kinley lived. Verna had taken Joy there twice. Sue was the same age as Verna but she lived alone in one of the smaller project housing units. Once Joy asked Verna how Sue could afford to live there alone. Verna said Sue worked. Later Joy found out Sue was a prostitute. Joy knocked on Sue's door. No one answered. Joy knocked again. A voice yelled through the door.

"Who is it?"

"It's Joy."

"I don't know no Joy."

"I am looking for Verna."

The door opened. Sue stood there in a nasty looking robe. It took a few minutes for her eyes to show recognition.

"Oh you Verna's baby sister. Come in sugar. Excuse the mess. I'm working."

Joy heard a male voice from the back bedroom call out to Sue.

"Wait a minute honey," Sue snapped. "You're gonna get yours."

11

Sue looked at Joy. "What can I do for you sugar?" "Nothing wrong is it, Where is Verna?"

Joy began to cry.

"What's wrong honey? Is Verna alright?"

"I don't know," Joy managed to say. "Verna left home. She said she was coming here."

"I ain't seen Verna but don't worry about her. You know it ain't safe for you to be out here walking around by yourself. Go on home now and I will find Verna and tell her to get in touch with you. She must have known I was working. Verna won't come over if she thinks I am working. You know she hates it when I work. I promise I will find Verna."

"Promise?"

"I promise."

JOY

The next day the word was all around the projects. Sue Kinley
was murdered by a John. She was found in her apartment. She had
been stabbed multiple times. Joy had not heard the news. As she
sat at home, she thought of Verna. She was getting very scared.
Where could Verna be? Was she o.k. She hoped Sue would keep
her promise and find Verna. Joy was snapped out of her thoughts
as she heard her Mama speak.

"Verna better not bring her black behind in this house." Mama
was talking to Stepdaddy.

Joy was depressed and hungry. She realized that she had not eaten
since Verna had left. Dinner was ready but Stepdaddy was home.

Joy was not ready to face Stepdaddy. She sat on her bed holding the Bible Verna had given her. Stepdaddy came to the bedroom door. He had a strange look on his face.

"Come eat."

Joy did not want to be near Stepdaddy but her hunger and the smell of fried chicken was overwhelming. She decided she would eat and quickly return to her room. She spent most of her time alone in her room. Looking out of her bedroom window hoping to see a familiar face walk by. Hoping to hear a familiar voice saying get your stuff let's go. If only she could see that rich dark skin and slanted eyes. She only saw unfamiliar faces. Joy looked at a picture of Verna on the dresser. Verna was leaning against a tree with a coke in her hand. The picture was taken by Sue Kinley a couple of months ago. Joy looked at the picture and began to feel hope. She could hear Verna say to her you are my joy in the morning. She smiled. Joy heard Stepdaddy's loud voice interrupt her pleasant thoughts.

"You better get in this kitchen and eat."

Joy sat at the table. Along with the chicken Mama had cooked collard greens, mash potatoes and corn bread. Mama cooked a lot.

Stepdaddy loved to eat. As Joy ate, she could feel Stepdaddy watching her. She ignored him. The food was good. She felt better. Verna's picture had given her hope. She knew Verna would come back for her as she promised. She watched as Junior and Precious put on their coats. Precious was excited.

"We are going to the movies."

"Yeah, Junior added. Joy get your coat."

"No," Mama snapped. "I want Joy to stay here and clean the dishes."

It was not uncommon for Mama to take Precious and Junior out. Junior looked sad.

"I want to stay home, Mama."

"Boy, don't play with me get your butt out that door."

Joy loved Junior. Lately he had become distant. She could tell he missed Verna. She watched as Mama took Junior and Precious out the door. It was strange how Junior looked back at her as he walked out the door. He looked so sad. Joy walked to the kitchen and began to wash the dishes. She did not want to be left alone with Stepdaddy. She felt someone watching her. Joy turned around to see Stepdaddy looking at her with a strange look on his face.

"Joy, bring me a beer."

"Yes sir." She quickly brought him a beer.

He grabbed her wrist.

"Do you love Stepdaddy?"

Joy could smell the alcohol on his breath.

"I said do you love Stepdaddy?"

Joy tried to pull away. "Please Stepdaddy leave me alone."

"Show me you love Stepdaddy."

Joy could feel the anger in her. "I hate you Stepdaddy, I hate you Stepdaddy, I hate you Stepdaddy."

He slapped her in the mouth. "Shut up before I kill you."

Joy continued to scream hysterically. "I hate you, I hate you, I hate you."

Joy felt an intense pain. Then there was complete darkness. When she awoke she was on her bed naked. Stepdaddy was standing over her. He was naked. Joy tried to run away. Stepdaddy grabbed her and threw her on the bed. He laid his full body on her.

Joy was dizzy. "Please Stepdaddy don't do this."

Joy tried to scream but Stepdaddy stuck his tongue down her throat. She started gagging. Stepdaddy pinched her breast so hard she cried out in pain. She had to do something. Joy bit down hard on Stepdaddy's lip. Stepdaddy let out a loud agonizing scream. Stepdaddy was furious. He was in a rage. He grabbed Joy's legs and spread them wide. She tried to kick but his weight was too much for her. Joy screamed with all her might. Stepdaddy stuck his dirty sock in her mouth. Joy felt the most excruciating pain. All she could think of was Verna and then she passed out. When Joy awoke she felt pain all over her body. Her door was open. Stepdaddy was gone but she could smell him. She was cold and suddenly she realized that she was naked. The reality of what had happened struck her. She opened her mouth to scream but no sound came out. She tried to sit up. The pain was unbearable. Joy did not hear anyone in the house. She did not know how much time had passed. She made it to her dresser and managed to put her robe on. She slowly walked to her door. She peeped out. Stepdaddy was gone. She slammed her bedroom door and locked it. This was a violation of Stepdaddy's rule. He said this was his house and nobody better ever lock a door around here but him.

Joy never understood this because Mama bought the house with money from her and Verna's Daddy. He had a small insurance policy. Joy also knew that her Mama received a check for her and Verna but she was never given any money. She dared not question Mama about the check. Joy felt so weak. She made it back to the dresser. She saw the picture of Verna. She grabbed the picture and smashed it on the floor. Verna looked back at her under what looked like a million pieces of glass. Verna was smiling.

Joy must have sat on the bed for hours staring in space. She noticed she was bleeding. She could not cry anymore. She heard Mama, Precious, and Junior come in the house. She waited until they went to bed. Joy went to the bathroom located in the hall way. She took a shower and then a hot bath. The water was so hot it burned her skin but she could not feel it, only numbness. She went back to her bedroom but returned to the bathroom to take another hot shower. She wondered why Mama did not say anything to her about the water running in the bathroom. She was always complaining about the water bill. Joy slowly returned to her bedroom. She sat on the hard floor. She did not want to ever sleep in that bed again. She could still smell Stepdaddy. Joy thought to herself, I hate you Verna. Suddenly she knew what she had to do. She grabbed her book bag and packed a few items. Joy lifted the window to leave. She looked back at the room, their room. Hers and Verna's. They had spent so many nights talking, laughing, and crying in this room. So much pain had been shared in this room. Joy climbed out the window. She had only walked a few blocks before turning around and returning to their bedroom. She lifted the window and painfully climbed back in. Strangely the pain was not physical but emotional. Joy walked over to the broken picture of Verna on the floor. She looked at the picture. She spoke out loud. "I don't hate you Verna. I am going to find you." She put the picture in her bag. She began to leave again but remembered the Bible. The Bible was on the floor. She picked it up and placed it tenderly in her jacket pocket. She heard the front door open. She knew it was Stepdaddy. She quickly climbed out the window and never looked back.

VERNA

It had been four days since Verna left home. She decided to rent a cheap hotel for a few days. She had a few dollars saved from braiding hair. Her plan was to stay with Sue until she could find a real job and make it on her own. Staying with Sue would allow her to save enough money so she could rent a room for herself and Joy. She thought about Joy a lot, almost every minute. She wondered if she had done the right thing leaving Joy behind. They had never been separated. She convinced herself that she had done the right thing for now. She did not want Joy living in the bottom in an apartment where prostitution was constantly going on. She tried to convince Sue to stop. Sue stated she had no other way to make quick money. Her philosophy was, if she was going to give it away free, she might as well get paid for it. She knew that Joy had a roof over her head and food to eat. Things she could not provide for her right now. She wanted Joy to finish school, besides what could go wrong. She had no way of knowing that as she was thinking this Joy was being raped by Stepdaddy.

As Verna approached the apartment where Sue lived, a feeling that something was wrong began to engulf her. She did not like the fact that her best friend was a prostitute. She told Sue many times about the dangers of prostituting. Sue would not listen. Prostitution was common among the young girls living in the bottom. Some of them had pimps. Sue said she was not giving her money to no man. Verna thought now would be the perfect time for her to convince Sue to go straight. They could look for a job together. Verna thought about how much fun it would be if they could find a job together. They had been friends since grade school. Sue had a rough life. She was raised by an alcoholic father after her Mother deserted her when she was seven. Sue had no brothers or sisters. Her Father never paid her any mind. He would feed her but mostly he ignored her and she pretty much raised

herself. She and Verna quickly formed a close bond. They were as

close as sisters. Verna knocked on Sue's door. Something did not

feel right.

"Hey you," A voice from behind startled Verna.

Verna turned to face a stout police officer.

"What's your name?" The police officer asked in an intimidating

tone. Before Verna could respond, the officer pointed his finger in

Verna's face.

"Do you know the girl who lives here?"

"Yes, she is my friend."

The officer continued to point his finger in Verna's face. He

continued to ask Verna questions.

"What do you know about her? When was the last time you saw

her? Did you know she was a prostitute?"

Verna was caught off guard. She thought Sue must have gotten

busted.

"She is my friend," Verna repeated.

The officer looked disgusted.

"She was your friend."

Verna became frightened. She tried to push past the officer who grabbed her by the arm.

"Your friend was a whore and she was murdered."

"No," Verna whispered. There must be a mistake."

The officer snapped. "There is no mistake. This is what happens when you people" Verna did not wait for the officer to finish. She took off running.

"Wait," the officer yelled. "I'm not finished with you."

Verna did not stop. She ran until she could not run anymore. The police officer did not follow her. She sat on the curb of a street known for prostitution. She had seen Sue stand on these streets many nights.

"Are you alright," a voice asked?

Verna did not answer. She did not turn to see who it was. She continued to sit on the curb crying. Finally she stood up and started walking. Her best friend was dead. Somehow she knew that she could not allow herself to fall apart. Joy was depending on her. She had to be strong for Joy. She tried her best to think of Joy but she could not get Sue out of her mind. She knew she had to go somewhere and get her mind straight. She realized that she had nowhere to go.

She only had ten dollars left. She thought of how Sue made money. It seemed so easy. She imagined Sue dead and she thought of Joy. She could not do that. Verna walked to 5th and Lenox. This was where most of the bars and restaurants were located. None of the restaurants needed help and the bars who were hiring all wanted proof that Verna was 21. She had no proof to offer.

It was cold. The only thing that kept Verna from thinking of Sue was the cold brisk air. The temperature was dropping quickly. She saw an old abandoned car parked on a back street. Verna laughed a hysterical laugh. She had seen movies where people slept in cars. She never thought it would happen to her. The car was an old Chevy. It was stripped bare. One of the front windows was smashed. There was glass all over the front seat. Verna sat in the back seat of the car. The car was filthy but she had no choice. She did not want to freeze to death. The car gave little protection against the cold, but at least she was out of the rain that had begun to fall. She knew that she would have to find better shelter soon.

She tried to fight down a wave of hysteria. She began to laugh.

Verna thought this is really messed up. All I need now is for it to

start snowing. Verna began to laugh again. She began to sing an

old rhyme from childhood. "Rain, rain go away little Verna wants

to play." She began to laugh again. She knew she was very close

to becoming hysterical, but she could not help herself. She began

to count and take deep breaths. Verna relaxed as she began to

regain her sanity. Suddenly she thought about the Salvation Army.

It was only a block away. She could have kicked herself. She

should have gone there to begin with. As Verna stepped out of the

Chevy, it began to snow.

Verna walked up to the old worn building that served as the local

Salvation Army. As she approached the desk, an elderly white

lady looked up at her.

"Can I help you young lady?"

"Yes, I need a room."

The old lady's tone was nasty.

"Well, I am sorry we are full."

"But I have nowhere to go."

"Yeah, you and a million others." The lady snapped. "How old are you anyway?"

"I am eighteen," Verna lied.

"We can squeeze you in tomorrow."

Verna was almost in tears. "What about tonight?"

The old lady snapped again "Look young lady, we have every bum, whore, junkie and Lord knows who else in here tonight. Everyone is looking for shelter."

Verna looked at the old lady. "Yeah Lord knows."

As Verna turned to leave, the old lady called her back. Her attitude seemed to have changed.

"I tell you what. The best I can do is give you a blanket and a cot until tomorrow. Then I will see about you getting a bed."

The old lady rang a bell. A young black girl of about twenty came out from the back.

The old lady's nasty attitude was back. She snapped at the young girl.

"Set this girl up with a cot and blanket."

27

Verna followed the girl to the back of the building. It opened up into an open floor. It reminded Verna of her school gym without the basketball hoops. There were cots lined up very closely. There were people everywhere, including some children.

The young girl introduced herself to Verna.

"What's up folks, they call me Rah Rah. That old hag someone is gonna kick her old white butt one day and it might just be me. I help out around here for a guaranteed three hots and a cot. To tell you the truth it really ain't worth it." Rah Rah led Verna to a bunk located in the middle of the room. "Sorry you in the middle but it is all that is left. I am surprised the old witch let you in. If you need anything holler."

Verna's cot was beside an old black man of about sixty-five. He had grey hair, a grey beard, and grey watery eyes. Even his complexion had a grayish tint. He smelled of old stale alcohol. Verna found herself staring at the old drunk's eyes. Suddenly, the old man pointed at Verna. His eyes seemed to show a sign of recognition.

"You," he whispered.

"Excuse me sir," Verna stammered.

"You," he said a little louder.

Verna was frightened.

"I don't know you sir."

The man started yelling. "You! You! You!"

There was a girl on the other side of Verna. She looked about twelve years old.

"Shut up Old Moe," the girl snapped.

She looked at Verna.

"Never mind him. He ain't got good sense. We gonna have to get him a drink so he won't be yellin all night."

She called over to a young man of about nineteen. He was leaning against the wall smoking a cigarette.

"Yo Jay, you still got that fifth of gin with ya?"

"Yeah," Jay replied. "You want a taste cuz?"

"Naw, but old man Moe seeing the devil again."

Verna watched as Jay walked over to the young girl.

"I ain't giving up my gin for nobody. You can have a taste but Moe ain't getting nothing from me. Who the devil this time?"

The young girl looked at Verna.

"What's your name?"

Verna was surprised.

"Who me?"

The girl laughed. "No, yo mammy."

Jay cut in.

"You mean Old Moe thinking this pretty young thang the devil?"

He held his head back and let out a loud startling laugh.

"You mean Old Moe," he was laughing so hard he could not finish his sentence.

"You mean Old Moe thinking this pretty thang the devil?"

He handed Old Moe the bottle of gin. "We can't have Old Moe thinking this pretty thang is the devil. Drink up cause you sure is crazy as the devil."

Jay sat on Verna's cot and looked at her long and hard.

"You sure have pretty eyes miss thang what is your name?"

Verna looked at Jay. He was the most handsome guy she had ever seen. He was tall and thin. He had creamy skin the color of a peanut shell. Jay looked at her with slanted sleepy eyes. When he smiled he showed a set of white even teeth.

"My name is Verna." She stammered.

Looking at him made her forget about all her problems.

Jay smiled.

"As you heard my name is Jay." He pointed to the young girl.

"This little loud mouth is my cousin Dee. What a pretty thang like you doing in a run down building like this on a cot in a room full of nobodies?"

Verna's eyes began to water. She fought down the wave of hysteria that she had experienced earlier in the abandoned car. She felt the need to tell someone. Suddenly she blurted out to Jay everything that had happened in the past few days.

Jay shook his head. He looked at Old Moe.

"Give me back that bottle old man. This girl needs it more than you."

At the mention of returning the bottle of gin, Old Moe stopped mumbling to himself. He jumped up and ran out the door into the cold night.

Jay jumped up from the cot. "Well I'll be. If it wasn't so cold I would go get my bottle."

Jay looked at Verna.

"What are you going to do?"

"I don't know. I have nowhere to go. I can't go home and I don't want to stay here."

Dee cut in. "Why don't you come and stay with me and Jay? We have a place."

Jay looked deep into Verna's eyes. "Now that ain't a bad idea."

Verna began to feel warm inside. "I don't understand. If you have a place then why are you here?"

"Well," Jay said. "We do have a place to lay our head on 35th street. We were not able to hustle up enough money to keep the heat on, so on cold nights like this we crash here at the center."

"I don't know," Verna said.

"Whatever pretty lady, but it looks like to me that you don't have too many options. Now you can stay here in this dump or me and cuz can set you up with a hustle and help you get started."

No one had called Verna pretty lady before.

"Yes, I will come with you but I don't want to hustle. I will find a legit job."

"Like I said," Jay replied. "Whatever, me and cuz got a little somethin somethin coming in tomorrow morning. We should be able to get the heat back on. I tell you what; tomorrow around noon meet me and cuz at O'Neil's coffee shop off of Fourth Avenue. We should be straight by then." That night in a cold, noisy, overcrowded Salvation Army building, Verna slept and dreamed about a tall handsome prince with slanted sleepy eyes.

The next morning Verna awoke at 6:00a.m. She looked around, but did not see Jay or Dee. She wondered what kind of business a young man and child could have so early in the morning.

"You," A loud voice interrupted her thoughts.

Verna turned to see that the old drunk had returned.

"You," he shouted!

"Oh shut up," Verna screamed. "I am not the devil. Just shut up you old drunk!"

People in the room began to wake up.

"I don't care what you are, a sleepy voice shouted, both of you shut up before I knock the devil into somebody!"

Old Moe started to mumble and point at Verna. She could not take it anymore. She grabbed her small bag. As she headed out the door into the cold, she passed Rah Rah at the front desk arguing with the old white woman from the night before.

Verna still had six hours before meeting Jay and Dee. She was hungry but afraid to spend her last ten dollars. She ducked into a laundromat to stay warm. She began to feel nauseated. As she sat on the bench, she thought about Sue and how she would miss her best friend. Suddenly a feeling of dread overcame her. She knew she had to check on Joy. It was 7:30a.m. Joy would be getting ready for school. Verna went to the wall pay phone. She dialed the number. On the third ring, Stepdaddy answered the phone. Verna hung up. She sat in the laundromat for another hour. She could not overcome her feeling of dread. She knew it had something to do with Joy. She dialed the number a second time. Stepdaddy answered again. Verna Paused.

She heard Stepdaddy. "Who is this?"

"Verna, can I speak with my sister?"

"No!" he yelled into the phone.

Verna heard him slam the phone down then a dial tone. She
dropped to the floor and cried.

It was 10:00a.m. Verna was hungry. She decided to go to
O'Neill's early and get something to eat. She ordered bacon, eggs
and some water. Noon time came and went but she saw no sign of
Jay or Dee. She sat looking out the window sipping water. At
1:00p.m. She decided that they must not be coming. Tears of
desperation began to fall again. She heard a voice.

"Are you alright?"

Verna looked up from where she was sitting to face an older white
man.

"Yes sir," Verna managed to say.

The white man seemed vaguely familiar.

"This is the second time in two days I have had to ask you if you
are alright."

"I don't believe I know you, sir."

"The first time I saw you, you were sitting on a curb crying
hysterically."

35

Verna vaguely remembered a voice asking her if she was o.k. the day she found out about Sue.

"Can I help you with something," he asked?

Verna could not stop the tears. "I need a job."

"How old are you?"

"I am twenty-one," Verna lied.

The man looked disappointed. "I could use someone to run the register and clean from time to time, but I can not hire you."

"Why," Verna begged.

"Because I can not use someone who is not straight with me. Can you be straight with me?"

"Yes," Verna replied.

"So how old are you?"

"I am seventeen."

"You know young lady that I serve beer in here."

"Yes," Verna said as she grabbed her bag and began to walk out.

"Wait," he shouted after her. "What did you say your name was?"

"What difference does it make?"

"If you are going to be working for me, I think I should know your name."

Verna smiled for the first time in days, "Thank You sir."

"I will need you everyday from noon until 6:00p.m. Pay is only minimum wage."

Verna thought about Joy. "You don't know how much I needed this."

"I think I do," he replied. "You can start tomorrow. Call me O'Neill."

Verna left O'Neill's feeling relieved. She found herself walking back towards the Salvation Army Center. She hated going back but it was the only choice she had. It was only 2:00p.m. The temperature had already started to drop. Maybe she was early enough to get a room this time. As Verna walked up to the center she was startled by a voice.

"Yo baby, what's happenin?" Verna turned around. It was Dee. "What ya standing there looking stupid for, come on."

Verna was surprised. "I thought y'all had forgotten me."

"No baby we ain't forgot ya. Our business just took a little longer but we got some money honey and we ready to partay."

"Where is Jay?" Verna asked looking around for him.

"He finishing up with business. He sent me to get ya. I figured you would come back to the center." Check this out, Dee continued, enough of all the talk we got some heat, some eats, some smoke, and some drink. Come on if ya coming because it is cold as a mug out here. Don't think I won't leave your butt right here."

Verna laughed. "O.K., but how did a little girl like you get so hip?"

"Look," Dee said. "I know I am fly, but if this thang is gonna work, you gonna have to learn to keep your mind off of me, let's roll baby."

Verna could not help but like Dee. She was tiny and wore a baseball cap that made her look like a little boy. She had the same slanted dreamy eyes that her cousin had. She also had white even teeth and the same peanut colored complexion. When she smiled she had two of the deepest dimples Verna had ever seen. Something about Dee made Verna want to protect her. She was just a baby trying to survive in an adult world. Verna wondered what her story was.

Dee and Verna approached a run down apartment building located in the worst section of the bottom.

'This is it," Dee said. "It ain't much, but it is home."

"I'll take it," Verna said.

"We on the fourth floor, but you gonna have to walk because we ain't got no elevator." Dee laughed at her own humor.

When Dee and Verna walked into the apartment, Jay was sitting on an old couch talking on the phone. Verna heard him speak to the person on the line. "I got to go, Too Short. My little cuz just came in. Give me some time to think on that, later." Jay hung up the phone.

"Well, well, well," Jay said. "Miss Thang welcome pretty lady. "It ain't much, but make yourself at home."

Something warm in Verna began to stir up again. She felt comfortable here.

"I got a job at O'Neill's. I will help out as much as possible."

"That's cool," Jay said. But if business keeps going the way it has been, we may not need your help. Save your money for you and your sister."

"What kind of business is it," Verna asked?

"It is not a business. It is a hustle. I will tell you about it soon enough. Let's just chill now."

"Can I ask you how you and Dee managed to be on your own?"

Jay hesitated. It was obvious he was not used to talking about himself.

"We used to live here with our Grandmother who raised us from babies because our Mothers, her daughters, were too sorry to take care of us. Grandma died two years ago. It has been me and Dee here since then."

"But, Dee is just a baby."

Dee spoke up. "I ain't no baby. Jay tell her I ain't no baby."

"Calm down cuz. Verna will come to know you in time. Verna you and your little sister can make it just like me and Dee have made it for two years and we have done just fine. Actually longer than that because Grandma had been very sick for the last few years of her life. Diabetes ain't no joke. That, plus the stress of trying to care for us at her age. Still we managed to get by. With the right hustle anybody can get by."

"But why hustle," Verna asked? "Why not find a real job?"

"Let's get one thing straight right now," Jay said. "I ain't slaving for nobody. If you choose to work down at O'Neill's for the white man then that is your perogative, but in a couple of years me and cuz will be straight. I'm taking us out of this bottom."

Verna could see she had struck a nerve.

Jay stood up. "Enough of this talk. Dee roll up a blunt. I will get the food. I bought Chinese. How does that sound?"

"Sounds good to me," Dee said.

"Me too," Verna echoed.

Verna had smoked marijuana with Sue in the past, but she only smoked it once in a while. Tonight she felt like she needed to forget her troubles. They smoked two blunts, ate the Chinese food, and finished off a bottle of cheap wine. Verna's troubles were quickly forgotten.

JOY

Joy did not know much about living on the streets. She was not a
sheltered child, but was never one to hang out in the streets or
know a lot of people. Joy had no money, no food, and no shelter.
Most of all, she was all alone. There was no way she could ever
go home even if it meant she had to die on the streets. She knew
she had to find Verna. She would never stop until she found her. It
was cold. Joy walked into a local bus station for warmth. She
must have fallen asleep because she awoke to a light tap on her
shoulder. She looked into the face of an elderly black woman. The
woman tenderly looked down at Joy. She had a look of concern
on her face.

"Child what you doing here by yourself?"

"I am waiting for the bus, mam."

"And what bus might that be pray tell?"

Joy stuttered. She could not bring herself to lie to this elderly woman.

"I, I, I'm trying to get warm, mam then I am going to look for my sister."

The elderly woman could see that the child was frightened.

"Where do you live, child?"

Before Joy could answer a tall white police officer walked over to them. He addressed the elderly black woman.

"Who is this Mae. Do we have another runaway?"

Joy wanted to run, but she was too frightened. Her legs seemed frozen.

"No," Mae said. "This here my grandbaby come to walk me to work this morning."

The police officer continued to address Mae.

"Mae, you know you have work to do and can't have your relatives sitting around here all the time."

"She about to leave."

The police officer walked away mumbling.

"Why did you do that," Joy asked?

"I'm a Christian woman, but I have not always lived a Holy life. I used to be young and foolish hanging out on the streets thinking I was having a good time. Once upon a time child, I suffered. I won't go into details, but I can say, watching you I recollect a time in my life when I needed help and no one helped me. By the grace of God he brought me out and showed me the way to righteousness. But it is a hard world out there and I think back, if someone had helped me, then maybe I would have been spared some of the heartaches. I did not know about God then and Satan was dragging me deeper and deeper into the pit of hell. I always believed that one day the time would come for me to help someone. Now it looks like to me child you calling for help and I am going to help you as best as I can. I feel like the Lord sent you my way so I can help you. You can't sit around here, but I want you to come back so I can help you."

Joy was touched by the old woman's compassion for her. She never had a Grandmother and often imagined how it would be to have one. She did not know this woman, but for some reason she trusted her.

"I have to look for my sister," Joy said in desperation.

"Listen child you go and look for your sister, but be careful because the Bottom is dangerous and you don't look like you from here. You come on back at 4:00p.m. I get off and if you find your sister you bring her back too, you hear?"

"Yes mam."

Joy stepped out of the bus station into the cold. She was hungry but her only concern was to find Verna. She knew Verna had to be in the bottom somewhere. She saw two young black girls standing on the corner. Joy reached into her pocket and pulled out the picture of Verna.

"Excuse me," she said. "I am looking for my sister. Do you know Verna Edwards?"

She showed them the picture. Both girls shook their heads no.

Joy walked by a place called O'Neill's. The smell of breakfast cooking made her mouth water. Standing in front of O'Neill's Joy experienced a strange feeling of familiarity. This feeling made her think of Verna. She had a strong urge to go inside and ask about Verna, but she shook off the feeling and continued walking. She wanted to cover as much of the streets as possible.

Joy was exhausted and hungry but mostly sad. No one had heard of or seen Verna. It was four o'clock. She decided that she would return to the bus station and look for the old woman. She needed someone to talk to. Maybe the old woman could let her work for some food. When Joy arrived at the bus station, Mae was standing outside. As Joy approached, Mae gave a sigh of relief.

"There you are sugar. I was worried about you. You look like something the cat dragged in. Lord have mercy child, you better come with me."

Joy was too tired to complain. She followed Mae like a lost puppy. The memories of the past night began to haunt her. They came to an old, but well kept small house. Joy was not surprised that the house was clean and neat. The flower furniture was old, but well taken care of. There was a color television, an old record player, as well as an antique looking china cabinet in the living room. To the right Joy could see a small cozy kitchen. There was no door just an opening. This allowed Joy to see a small table

surrounded by four chairs. Joy watched as Mae took off her coat

and put down her bag.

"Have a seat child and get yourself warm while I fix us something

to eat."

Joy sank down onto the old couch. It was very soft. She laid her

head back and slept.

Joy woke up startled Mae was screaming and shaking her.

"Wake up child! What's wrong?"

Joy was shaking. Her face was wet with tears.

Mae was speaking to Joy softly. "You were screaming no

Stepdaddy. Child what happened to you? Who is Stepdaddy?"

Mae was softly telling Joy to let it out.

Joy began to work her mouth, but nothing would come out. The

words were too painful to say.

"Listen child," Mae said. "I don't know what has happened to

you, but I feel that whatever happened must be eating your little

soul away. I can help you. Let me help you baby."

Mae grabbed Joy and held her. Joy tried to push her away.

"No," she screamed. "I am dirty."

Mae was sixty five years old, but somewhere in her she found the strength to hold on to this hysterical child. She softly spoke to Joy.

"Let it out honey."

Joy continued to fight and cry.

Mae continued to hold on.

"That's it, release it baby."

Finally Joy stopped fighting and held on to Mae.

"Help me she cried. Please help me."

Mae held on to the child until she cried herself to a fitful sleep.

There was something about this brown skinned girl that touched Mae. Mae knew it the first time she saw her asleep in the bus station. She felt with all her heart that God had sent this child for her to take care of. She knew that something terrible had happened to Joy. She felt that Joy had run away from something horrible and as long as she could help it, Joy would never have to return to whatever or whoever had hurt her so deeply.

When Joy woke up it was dark outside. Mae was sitting in a chair reading a Bible. She spoke to Joy.

"I know you have to be starving."

Joy stood up. "I better go."

Mae stood up. "I am not going to let you go until you eat something. Don't disrespect me. Do you hear me child?"

Mae sensed that Joy was not one to disrespect adults. She would have to use this until the child was comfortable. Somehow she knew that she could not let the child leave her house.

Joy sat down to a meal of hot home made beef and vegetable soup along with fresh hot biscuits.

The old woman watched the child eat.

"Child you must not ate in days."

"No mam," Joy replied.

Mae scooped more hot soup into Joy's empty bowl.

"Let's get this straight. Call me Grandma Mae."

"I can't."

"Why?"

"Because I am not comfortable calling you that. You are not my Grandma."

"O.K." the old woman said. "Just call me Ms. Mae. We will take it from there."

Joy stood up again. "Thanks for the food Ms. Mae, but I have got to go look for my sister now."

Mae was determined not to let Joy leave. "There ain't no way I am going to let you leave tonight. Stay tonight and we will start fresh tomorrow morning."

"But this is not my home," Joy said.

"Child do you have a home?"

Joy hung her head. "All I got is Verna."

Mae hugged Joy. "Now you got me." Joy could not help but lay her head on Mae's soft shoulder.

As Joy slept, Mae remembered her life. So many memories that she had long forgotten came back to her. Something about this child made her remember her past. Mae grew up in a small Mississippi town. She grew up in a time of intense racial prejudice and strong moral beliefs within the black community. She was raised by her Mother and Grandmother. She could not remember her Father. She was told he left her Mother when Mae was only two years old for another woman. At thirteen, Mae became pregnant. She remembered how her Mother told her that she could not allow her to bring a baby into her household. Mae refused to tell them the father was a 23 year old son of one of their neighbors. Mae thought she was in love. He told her he would be there with her forever. When Mae told him she was pregnant, he told her he did not want to raise his child in a racist town and that he would go to Detroit to find a job and come back for her. Mae waited for two months. He never returned or sent a letter. Mae's Mother told her she would have to go away and have the baby and give the baby up. Mae refused to do this. Instead, at four months, she ran away to Detroit. She stole her Mother's money earned from washing other people's laundry. She used the money to buy a ticket to Detroit. She did not know where to find the baby's Father and found herself caught up in the world of teenage prostitution. When she got off the bus, there were pimps waiting at the bus stop. She had that throwaway child look and was immediately promised shelter. He said he would buy her food and clothes. At first he gave her clothes and jewelry. He took her to get her hair and nails done. He had other women who worked the streets. He told her he loved her. At first she did not have to work

the streets. She thought she was special. The pimp's love and kind

attitude quickly became violent. She told him about her

pregnancy. She was forced to work although she was pregnant.

She told herself she would run into her baby's Father and he

would take her away from the life. The pimp would beat her with

a wire clothes hanger. One day he beat her so bad; she miscarried

and was force to lie in her own blood for hours. She was finally

taken to the hospital by some other prostitutes who left her at the

hospital emergency room entrance. This was a wake up call for

Mae, but she could not go home. She was afraid of the Pimp. He

would try to find her if she ran. At the hospital Mae met the

chaplain. He told her that God loved her. She told him that she

was a sinner and had done a lot of bad things and that God could

not love her. The chaplain asked Mae if she believed in God. She

told him she did. He asked her if she believed in the Bible. She

told him yes. He asked her if he could show her in the Bible that

God loved her even as a sinner would she believe it and change.

She promised him that if he could show her that in the Bible, she would accept his help and turn her life to God from that moment on.

The Chaplain opened his Bible and asked her to read with him Romans chapter 5 and verse 8. Mae slowly read, "But God commendeth His love toward us; in that while we were yet sinners, Christ died for us." As Mae remembered this, tears came to her eyes. That night she accepted God's love and Christ as her Savior. The Chaplain helped her get into a shelter for homeless prostitutes. The only one of its kind in the entire country. The shelter helped her to get a GED and a part-time job. At 17 they helped her to get an apartment. She never ran into her baby's father. She did see the pimp from time to time, but it was as if he did not recognize her because he never said anything to her. She knew she was protected by God's love.

At 18, Mae met and married Benjamin Brown. He was a hard worker at the bus station where Mae worked part-time. At first, Ben was hired as a janitor. After working as a janitor for five years, Ben was able to take classes and become a bus driver. He did not care about her past. He told her if God had forgiven her who was he not to forgive her. He told her God has forgotten her past and does not remember it and so to him her past does not exist. Together they worked hard enough to put a down payment on their little home. When Ben died, only 8 years earlier, Mae had enough money from his insurance policy to pay off their house. There was also enough money left for Mae to live comfortably. She no longer needed to work, but did work two or three times a week just to get out of the house. She missed Ben and now that Joy had come into her life, she was looking forward to taking care of someone who needed her again.

The next morning, Joy awoke to the smell of frying fish, fried potatoes, and home made corn bread. She felt that this strange woman really cared about her. It felt good that someone cared. No one had ever cared about her but Verna. When she first awoke she had forgotten where she was. When she realized that she was not in her own bed, the memories of being raped and the loss of Verna returned. She walked into the kitchen to see Ms. Mae at the sink washing dishes.

Ms. Mae smiled at Joy. "Good Morning, did you wash up yet?"

"Not yet," Joy replied.

Mae walked to a closet and handed Joy a towel and wash cloth.

"Go wash. Breakfast will be ready in about twenty minutes."

Joy showered and changed into her one of only two set of clothing she brought with her. She made sure she dressed in the warmer outfit in anticipation of another cold day of searching for Verna. Her hair was a mess. Tears came to her eyes as she remembered that this was the day that Verna always pressed her hair. This was the first Tuesday in two years that Verna had not pressed her hair.

"Come on child," Ms. Mae called from the kitchen. "Let's get moving."

Joy sat down at the kitchen table. Mae noticed Joy staring at the food.

"Why you staring at the food child? Something wrong with it?"

"No mam, it looks good. Fried fish and potatoes are a dinner meal and a Sunday meal at that."

Mae laughed. "Not in this house. Fried catfish taste best when eaten in the morning. Caught yesterday by Sam."

"Who is Sam?"

"Sam is an old fool. He is my neighbor. He come around here and fix whatever is broken. Spends much of his time fishing. Always bringing me plenty of fresh fish, bless his heart."

Joy smiled. Sam sounded like a nice man.

Mae threw her hands up faking surprise. "Lord have mercy now look at that little miss went and smiled and such a pretty smile too."

Joy laughed. "Ms Mae, I really thank you for letting me stay here and feeding me, treating me real good, but I have to find my sister today."

"What if you don't find her?"

Joy started to cry. "I don't want to accept that."

"Honey I am sorry," Mae said. "This is something we have to talk about. Where on earth will you go, child?"

"I don't know where I will go."

"Can you go home?"

"I can never go home."

"Tell me why you can't go home."

Joy began to shake. "Because my Mother hates me and Stepdaddy raped me. "He raped me."

Mae could see the pain and anger in this child. She wished she could take some of the pain away.

Joy continued as tears of anger fell down her face. "He held me down and he-

Mae cut Joy off. "It's o.k. now."

"It's not o.k." Joy yelled! "Verna should have been there."

"It's o.k. to be angry," Mae said.

Joy continued to yell. "I hate Verna, I hate Verna!"

"Oh no child," Mae said.

"I do. I do hate her."

Joy broke down crying. "Where are you Verna?"

Mae held Joy. "It's alright to be angry at your sister but you don't hate her."

"I don't know where she is. She could be dead."

"Don't worry we will find your sister. Stay with me until we find her."

"I would like that."

Mae looked hard at Joy. "There is one condition. You will have to enroll in Faith Christian School."

"I have to find Verna before I can even think about going to school."

"Do you think your sister would want you to quit school?"

Joy remembered one of the last things Verna said to her was to stay in school.

"O.k., but I will never stop looking for my sister."

Because Mae had money from her husband's insurance policy and money saved from working part-time, Mae was able to send Joy to private school.

For the next several months Joy's days developed into a normal routine of going to Faith Christian School and eating dinner with Mae. After dinner, they both would walk the streets looking for Verna. When they came home, Joy would study into all hours of the night. Joy had found many friends at her new school. Sometimes they would help Joy look for Verna. Joy had also developed a special relationship with old man Sam. Sam had developed an instant liking for Joy. At first when he found out about Joy, he tried to convince Mae not to become involved. He told her she could not just take a child off the streets. But he soon found out that Mae was a stubborn old woman. She would not change her mind. Sam was glad he was not able to convince Mae to change her mind because if he had, he would have missed out on a special relationship. Sam watched day by day as Joy went out looking for her sister. Sam never said so but he had gone out on his own a couple of times to ask around about her sister. He truly believed that Joy's sister must be dead. He never said this because it was the only thing that kept the poor child going. It took a while for Joy to begin to trust Sam. Mae had said to give it time because she had been abused. Slowly Sam had seen the distrust in Joy's eyes turn into something special. Sam took Joy fishing with him on weekends. She would always talk about her sister. He could see the pain in Joy's eyes as she talked about her past life. Whatever it was that Mae saw in this child, he felt it too. He knew that Joy was their special child.

For the past several weeks, Mae had not been feeling well. Joy and Sam had decided to go grocery shopping for her. On the way back from the store, Sam and Joy approached a group of men standing on the corner drinking beer.

"Bums," Sam said. "Let's walk on the other side of the street."

As they were about to cross the street one of the men yelled Joy's name. Both Joy and Sam turned to face Stepdaddy approaching them.

Joy began to shake. It had been almost a year since the rape yet she was as frightened as if it was yesterday.

Sam sensed something was wrong. "What's wrong baby. Who is that man?"

"That's him. That's Stepdaddy."

"Is that the devil who raped you?"

Before Joy could answer Stepdaddy reached out and grabbed her arm. Joy smelled the familiar smell of alcohol on his breath.

"Come with me," Stepdaddy slurred.

Sam put down the groceries. "Wait a minute. Take your hands off my child."

Stepdaddy looked at Sam. "I don't know who you are old man, but this is my child."

"You hurt her."

"This is my child and I can do what I want to with her."

Sam watched in desperation as Stepdaddy dragged Joy off. Seeing Stepdaddy dragging off a screaming young girl seemed to sober the group of men who were drinking with Stepdaddy.

"Yo man," one of them yelled "What you doing. Leave that child alone."

"This is my child," he slurred. He continued to drag Joy. "Tell them baby. Don't you love Stepdaddy?"

At the mention of those words. Joy became hysterical.

Sam followed pleading. "Leave the child alone. You want money. I have money."

Stepdaddy stopped and threatened Sam. "Look old man, I will kill you."

Sam grabbed Stepdaddy's shirt and tried to pull him away from Joy. "Help me someone," he pleaded to Stepdaddy's drinking partners.

The three men dropped their heads in shame, but no one stepped forward to help Sam.

A blind rage came over Sam. This was his child and no one was going to hurt her again. Sam ran back to where he had dropped the grocery bag. He pulled out a bottle of apple juice. With all his strength he came down on the back of Stepdaddy's head. Sam and Joy watched as Stepdaddy sank to the ground. Sam grabbed Joy's hand, leading her home.

Sam picked up the grocery bag off the street. If they would have turned around they would have seen Stepdaddy weakly reach out his hands towards his friends for help. They would have also seen Stepdaddy's friends shake their heads pathetically, turn and walk away, leaving Stepdaddy bleeding on the street.

Sam and Joy had decided not to mention to Mae what had happened. They did not want to upset her.

Sam looked at Joy. "I don't think he will be bothering you again."

Joy looked up and smiled at Sam. "I love you."

"I love you too." This was the first time Sam had ever said these words in his 69 years of living.

Mae's condition seemed to get worst day by day. Joy had lived with Mae for over a year now. The past few days had been the first time since living with Mae that Joy had not made an effort to look for Verna. Instead she had sat by Mae's bed holding her hand and reading the Bible to her.

Mae squeezed Joy's hand. "You are special Joy. God sent you to me. He told me that you will be someone special. You will help a lot of people. Your sister is alive and you will see her again." She continued to squeeze Joy's hand. "Do you believe me, baby?"

Joy smiled at Mae. "I believe you mama and you will get well because I still need you."

Tears of Joy came to Mae's eyes.

Joy was concerned. "Why are you crying are you alright?"

"You called me mama. I finally got my baby. I will get better because now that I have my baby, I sure as hell can't leave now."

Joy was surprised. "Mama you cursed."

"God will forgive me this one time and anyway there is one thing I am sure of and that is there is a hell."

They both laughed.

Time passed. Joy learned that she was not dumb and ugly as Stepdaddy and her Mother made her out to be. Joy made good grades and had many friends. She finally found a place she could call home. The pain that had been a part of her life had diminished. What was left was a nagging ache. Joy knew she would never be at peace until she found her sister and only then would the ache go away. Joy became involved with school and church groups. Everyday she thought of Verna. She still had the little Bible Verna left with her. Every night before going to bed she would hold the Bible and pray with it in her hands. She asked God to bring her sister to her and protect her. Some days she would see a face in the crowd who looked like her sister. She would call out Verna's name, but it never turned out to be Verna. In spite of what Mama Mae had told her about seeing Verna again, she had begun to lose hope of ever seeing her sister again. Deep down inside, she felt as if she had lost Verna forever. Everything she did now was in memory of her sister. She thought to herself, since she could not be with Verna, she would make Verna proud of her. She had to believe that somehow, Verna would know that she did it all for her.

VERNA

One year had passed since Verna had moved in with Jay and Dee.
She enjoyed working at O'Neill's. O'Neill treated her so kind. Jay
would not take any money from Verna. She had managed to save
six hundred dollars. Verna was very worried about Joy. She had
called the house on several occasions. Stepdaddy or her Mother
would answer the telephone. Stepdaddy would always hang up on
her. Once she had pleaded with her Mother to let Joy come to the
telephone. Her Mother had told her that Joy did not want to talk to
her and to quit calling. Verna would not accept this. She told her
Mother that could not be true. Her Mother yelled at her in the
telephone and told her she was no longer a part of the family. She

stressed that Joy did not want to talk to her and told her not to call the house no more. Verna felt something was wrong. She had gone to the school but the teachers told her that Joy no longer attended the school. Verna was desperate. She knew what she had to do. Early on a school morning she had gone to the corner around the block from her Mother's house. She knew her brother Junior would walk to school this way. She spotted Junior approaching her in the distance. She yelled Junior's name. Junior looked as if he did not know who she was. She called him again.

"It's me, Verna!"

Junior ran to her at full speed and almost knocked her down. People stopped to stare. It seemed quite strange to see this light skinned curly hair boy hugging this tall dark brown young lady with the short afro.

"Walk with me, Junior, I need to talk to you."

As they walked Verna could sense that something was wrong.

"Where is Joy?"

"Joy is gone."

Verna tried to hold herself together. "Gone where?"

"I don't know."

"What do you mean you don't know?" Verna's voice began to crack.

"She left several days after you did. I swear I tried to find her but she was gone."

Verna felt as if she would fall. "Why didn't she wait? I told her to wait for me. She knew I was coming back."

"She could not wait" Junior said softly.

"Why?" Verna asked.

"I think my Father hurt her."

"Hurt her, how?"

Junior dropped his head. "I heard my Father tell Ma he made Joy a woman."

"Oh my God," Verna dropped down on the street.

Junior grabbed Verna's arm. "Get up off the street, Verna."

"Oh no!" Verna yelled. "Not Joy, not my Joy! Why! Why!"

Junior continued to try to pull Verna up. People were looking.

"It's my fault," Junior said.

Verna looked up at Junior. "No, Junior it's not your fault."

"I should have protected her." Junior began to walk away.

Verna picked herself up from the dirty street. "Wait, Junior!"

Junior began to run. Verna tried to catch him but his young legs were too fast for her.

As Verna slowly walked back to the apartment she shared with Jay and Dee, she could not stop the tears of anger.

Verna mumbled to herself. "You lied Stepdaddy. You said if I never told you would leave Joy alone."

Verna thought back to the times that she and Stepdaddy would somehow be left alone. Her Mother would take her sisters and brother to the movies. She would tell Verna to stay home and do some kind of house work. The first time Stepdaddy raped her, Verna yelled and threatened to tell someone. She told him he would not get away with what he had done to her. Stepdaddy told her if she did tell he would do the same thing to Joy. He told her if she wanted Joy safe then she better not open her big mouth. Verna had become hysterical, begging him not to hurt her sister. He made Verna promise to do whatever he wanted and never to tell. She promised and Stepdaddy smiled and promised never to touch Joy. She believed him.

Verna continued to mumble to herself. "You will pay for this Stepdaddy. I will get you."

Verna walked into the apartment and sank down on the old dirty rug on the floor.

Jay walked in carrying an armful of men's clothing. Verna found out months ago that this was Jay's hustle. He received stolen goods then sold them.

Jay walked over to Verna. "What's wrong with you? Why you sitting on the floor like that?"

Verna was quiet.

Jay held his hand out to her. "Look at me."

Verna looked up into his dark slanted eyes. She felt the familiar warmth that she felt every time she looked into his eyes.

Jay helped Verna off the floor. As Jay held on to Verna, she told him about all that had happened. She also told him about the many times Stepdaddy had raped her. She had never told anyone this before. There were many times during the day that Jay and Verna found themselves alone. Jay would allow Dee to run errands for him during the day. However, during these times, Jay

71

never once tried to touch Verna. She did not want him to let her go. She never knew that someone could hold her so tenderly. Jay stroked her hair.

"Let me love you."

Verna looked at Jay. "Make me forget."

Jay led Verna into the bedroom. Verna was nervous. She thought please let this be different. Verna never knew it could be like this. As Jay held her she cried.

"Why are you crying," he asked.

"Because I never knew it could be this good."

"It gets better," Jay said.

But for Verna things did not get better. She began to get high everyday. She missed work more and more. This was the only way she could cope with not knowing where Joy was and what had happened to Joy. She kept seeing Stepdaddy doing to Joy what he had done to her. Her only satisfaction was marijuana and making love to Jay. These were the only two things that made her feel happy. Whenever she was not doing these things, she would sit around in a state of depression.

Dee came in with a box of women shoes.

"Hey yo, what's up?"

Verna smiled at Dee. "Nothing much, what you got?"

"I got some shoes. Take a look at em before I unload them."

"Naw," Verna said.

"O.k., but I got some funky ones in here."

Verna could not help but to smile at this child whom she had come to care about so much. She wondered what type of future she had. She knew Jay really loved Dee, but she often wondered if he was doing the right thing. Dee was a straight up street hustler. She did not go to school. She smoked weed and drank. Verna had asked Jay about Dee going to school. He snapped at her telling her if Dee went to school then they would find out about them and take Dee from him and he straight up told Verna to mind her business.

Dee held up a shoe, "Whoa baby look at these shoes. Jay said for me to take em to Ms. Shirley. She gonna give me two hundred dollars for em. Jay said I can have the money. Wanna get high tonight?"

"Dee I been meaning to tell you, you are too young to be smoking and drinking. You need to leave the dope and alcohol alone."

"Look baby," Dee said. "I am tired of you trying to tell me what to do. Jay ain't never telling me what to do so chill out with that."

"Don't you want to go to school?"

Dee made a face at Verna. "Now I know you straight trippin. The only school I need is Jay and the streets, for real. I got to go ditch these shoes. They real hot, baby."

Verna felt an urgency. "Wait, I want you to think about what I said. I don't want anything to happen to you."

Jay walked in.

"Hey what's up, Dee I thought I told you to ditch those shoes. You know the heat is on. I want you to get rid of them before it gets dark."

"I am going," Dee said. "Verna the one holding me up. She starting on me again."

Jay became angry. "Look Verna let up off of Dee. I know what's best for her."

He looked at Dee.

"Dee get on over to Ms. Shirley with them shoes. She's expecting them tonight. She is good clientele and we don't want to disappoint her."

Dee quickly grabbed the box and headed out onto the streets.

"What's wrong with you," Verna asked.

"I'm just tired. Come rub my back."

"Got a blunt?"

"Yeah," Jay said handing Verna a blunt. "Fire it up."

"This is some good stuff" Verna said. "But it taste funny."

"It's laced," Jay said.

"What do you mean laced?"

"Don't worry about it. You're my woman right."

"Always."

"You know I would never give you anything to hurt you. This is going to make you feel real good. When we finish this, we going to make love all night long. You don't have to work tonight do you?"

Verna smiled. "I have to work, on you."

When Verna woke up it was 7:00p.m. She had missed work for the third time that week. She had begun to dabble in the money she had saved. She knew she was losing perspective. She knew she needed to get herself together. She picked up the phone and dialed O'Neill's.

"Hello O'Neill this is Verna. I missed work because I am having my period and cramps and stuff." This always seemed to quiet men up. She was sure he would not ask her any questions.

O'Neill surprised Verna. "Get down here right now. I need to talk to you."

"I took some medication for my cramps that make me drowsy." O'Neill's voice sounded upset. "I gave you a job when you needed one. I like you but if you don't come here now, you will not have a job." He hung up the phone.

"This sucks," Verna said.

Jay was lying beside Verna. He awoke to Verna getting dressed.

"What's wrong pretty lady?"

"I have got to go down and talk to O'Neill."

"I thought you did not have to work tonight."

"I never said I did not have to work."

Jay stretched. "Forget him. You don't have to work. I'm getting ready to get into something big."

Verna became alarmed. "Like what?"

"You don't have to know right now. This hustling is not bringing in enough money fast enough."

Verna began to stroke Jay's head. "Oh, but it is enough Jay. You are in deep enough."

Jay became angry. "Like I told you before," he said pulling away from her, I know what is best. I am the man around here and I will take care of Dee and you."

"Jay it is not safe for Dee to be on the streets so much. It's getting dark and she's not even home yet."

At the mention of Dee, Jay jumped up and slipped on some pants. "I have got to go find Dee. It is hot out there tonight. I will talk to you later."

"Let me walk with you," Verna asked.

"No, I have got to take care of a little business. I'll send Dee home. If she gets here before I find her, tell her to stay her little butt in the house."

After Jay left, Verna thought about Dee and Jay. They never talked much about their family. Whenever Verna brought it up, they quickly changed the subject. Verna could see that they had a special bond.

Jay took good care of Dee. Dee dressed in the latest styles. She never went hungry. Dee was very stubborn. She worshipped the ground Jay walked on. She wanted to make him proud. Dee was a good hustler. As much as Jay loved Dee, Verna could not understand why he would send her out on the streets to hustle. Verna had offered to work with Jay in order to keep Dee off the streets but Jay had told her no. Jay told Verna she was not made for the game. Dee had it going on. No one could resist her baby doll appearance. Jay never sent Dee out alone at night. He did most of the hustling at night himself. Dee always wanted to go with him. Verna laughed to herself thinking of how Dee would complain to Jay about leaving her home with boring Verna. Jay would laugh walking out the door, leaving Dee and Verna alone. Most of the time, they would sit around smoking weed and drinking wine. At first, Verna was uncomfortable getting high with a twelve year old, but after a while she just accepted Dee for who she was. Verna smiled thinking about Dee. She could hear her say, "Let's get busy." One time Verna had asked her to stop getting high so much. Dee's response was I have to deal with your boring butt.

Verna slowly got up, took a shower, and threw on a sweat suit. She did not feel like dealing with O'Neill but he had been so good to her. She did not want to seem ungrateful. Jay had left her a joint on the dresser. There was a note that said get right because I will be back tonight for so more good loving. Verna smiled. She loved Jay. He made her forget about Joy. Verna smoked half the joint. It tasted funny. It must be laced. What the heck it made her feel so good. This stuff is the bomb she thought.

When Verna walked into O'Neill's he did not look happy.

"What's up," she said.

"I see you are feeling better."

"Much better," Verna laughed. She was feeling real tipsy.

O'Neill looked very concerned. "Verna, I am not going to waste any time. I have noticed a change in you. I have not said anything, but you have been missing a great deal of time from work. When

79

you do come in, you have been high on something. Matter of fact, you are high now."

Verna became angry. "Are you accusing me of something?"

"No, I am concerned about you. If it had been any other employee, they would have been fired long ago."

"Don't do me any favors," Verna snapped.

O'Neill shook his head sadly. "I can't believe how much you have changed. I am willing to help you. That is why we are having this talk. I am giving you another chance."

Verna's anger escalated. "Another chance, who are you white man? I don't need any white man to give me nothing. I am out of here, Mister Charlie."

As Verna walked out, O'Neill remembered the sad, hurt child who had touched something in him that first day. He had taken a chance and hired her. "You are a very troubled child," he said to no one in particular. "A very troubled child."

Verna was very angry and she did not know why. In her heart she knew that O'Neill only wanted to help her. She could not believe she said those things to O'Neill. She felt bad. She knew she would

never be able to face him again. Her anger turned into depression.
What's wrong with me, she thought. She walked back to the
apartment. She lit the other half of the joint. "Let's get busy," she
said and laughed. As she smoked the joint, she could feel all her
problems slip away.

Jay came in two hours later. He was very upset. "Is Dee here?"

"No," Verna said becoming worried. "I thought she was with
you."

"I can't find her," Jay said almost in tears.

Verna grabbed her coat. "Let's go."

Verna and Jay looked all night. Exhausted they returned to the
apartment. The phone rang. Jay snatched it up. "Dee!"

There was a strange voice on the telephone. "This is the second
precinct police department. Do you know a Deidra Wilson?"

"Yes," Jay said. "What is it?"

"We picked her up for possession of stolen property and
possession of marijuana."

Jay was upset but he breathed a little better. His Dee was alive.

"What's the bail? Can I come and get her out?"

"I'm afraid not."

"Why?"

"She has been turned over to social services. You need to be in court Tuesday morning which is three days from now."

"O.k., I will be there," Jay responded.

"What's wrong," Verna asked in a panic.

"Dee has been picked up by the man."

Verna dropped her head in her hands. "What are we going to do?"

Jay sat down on the couch. He felt so lost. "All we can do is wait and see what happens in court. At least she is safe."

Jay stood up. "I have got to go hustle some money for bail."

Verna was confused. "Where are you going to get that kind of money?"

"Remember when I told you I was going to get into something big."

Verna shook her head yes.

"I have the chance to start selling crack. I can get my hands on a large amount and when that's gone, I can get some more."

"No Jay, not that. Anything but crack."

Jay continued to put his coat on. "Crack is no worst than any other drug. It is no worst for you. What do you think I laced the reefer with?"

"You gave me crack, Jay, why?"

"I gave it to you because I love you. I saw how depressed you were getting."

Verna could not believe it Jay had said he loved her. That made everything alright. He would never hurt her. "We will do whatever it takes to get Dee back. Whatever you do I am with you."

Tuesday morning Verna and Jay awoke early for court. For the past couple of days, they had sold close to a thousand dollars in crack. Verna was amazed at how fast and easy the money came. Jay was in good spirits. With a thousand dollars surely he would be able to get Dee back. When they arrived, Dee was sitting up in the front of the courtroom with two women. One of them looked vaguely familiar to Jay. She was very conservative looking with smooth paper bag brown skin. Her long hair was pulled back in a simple bun. She looked in her early thirties. "I know that lady,"

Jay whispered to Verna.

"She's very attractive," Verna said.

"All arise for the Judge," the bailiff said. Jay and Verna rose. Dee

looked at them and waved.

"Dee looks sad," Jay observed.

"Young man," the Judge said, "Are you the guardian of this

child?"

"Yeah," Jay said.

"Yes sir," to you young man and stand when you address this

court."

"Yes sir, I am her cousin."

"Who established guardianship," the Judge wanted to know?

Jay was confused. "We were raised by our Grandmamma. When

she died it became my responsibility to," "Young man," the Judge

cut in, I will ask you again, who established guardianship?"

"Our blood established guardianship," Jay yelled.

"Contain yourself young man," the Judge ordered. "You may

have a seat. I rule that guardianship has not been established. You may approach the bench Mrs. Ward." "Are you the caseworker assigned to this case?"

"Yes, I am Your Honor."

"And what are your findings, Mrs. Ward?"

"Your Honor, I find that this child is a victim of her environment, which includes non-supervision, no authority figure, and a negative role model. Your Honor, the child has been allowed to run wild. She can't even speak proper English and has not been in school in years. We found traces of marijuana in her system.

"Your Honor, this is not the child's fault."

"Whose fault is it," the Judge asked?

Mrs. Ward pointed to Jay. "Your Honor it is the fault of this young man. Who has not been responsible enough to care for this young child."

"Now wait a minute," Jay interrupted.

"Young man," the Judge ordered. "If you can not contain yourself you will be removed from this court."

Jay sat down. "I can't believe this," he whispered to Verna.

"Ms. Ward," the Judge continued, "What are your recommendations?"

"Your Honor, there is no question that this child must be taken out of the environment in which she has resided."

"Do you suggest we place this child in detention?"

"No sir, detainment would not benefit this child. She needs to be placed in a loving, responsible and structured environment."

"So you are recommending foster care?"

"Sir, we were able to locate the child's Mother. She left the child in the care of her Mother ten years ago. When she tried to reclaim the child five years ago her Mother had moved."

"You liar," Jay thought.

"Your Honor," Ms Ward pointed to the young lady sitting beside Dee, this is the child's Mother. She lives in Virginia Beach, Virginia. She has a job as a librarian. Her husband works for a well known law firm and they have a two year old son. Sir, she is able to raise this child in an upper middle class environment. I would like to strongly recommend that since this is the child's Mother and custody has never legally been taken away from her, that you release the child in her custody."

The Judge stood. "I will consider your recommendation. Court will be adjourned for one hour."

Jay jumped up. "Wait a minute. I have not said anything in my behalf."

"Young man," the Judge said. "That will not be necessary."

Jay yelled at Dee's Mother. "You liar. You never came back for Dee!"

"Security remove this man from my court," the Judge ordered.

"Don't put your hands on me," Jay yelled.

Verna grabbed Jay's arm and led him out the court room. He was so angry.

"Jay," Dee yelled!

Dee ran into Jay's arms.

"I'm sorry Jay."

"It's not your fault, Dee."

"I got caught, Jay."

"Don't worry about that now," Jay said.

The caseworker and a police officer walked up to Jay and Dee.

She spoke to Dee. "Deidra until the Judge makes his decision you are to remain with us."

"I ain't going nowhere," Dee said. "I just want to talk to Jay and Verna for a while."

"Come with me now," the caseworker said. "If you don't come now, we will have to place you in a holding cell until the Judge returns with his decision."

"Go with them Dee," Jay said. "I will see you later."

Dee kissed Jay and Verna. She slowly walked away. Dee's Mother came out of the court room. She stopped in front of Jay. "Try to understand," she said.

Jay looked at her with hatred in her eyes. "You lied. You don't care about Dee."

"You are wrong," she said. "I care about Deidra. If you care you would let her go. She needs to be off the streets in a real family. She needs to be in school like other little girls. She needs to be a little girl, Jay. Let her go."

"I am her only family," Jay said. "You left her when she was a baby. You don't even know her and she does not know you."

"Listen," she said, staring Jay in the eyes. "You were only a small child when I left. I had no choice. My Mother, your beloved Grandmother, put me out. I had nothing. Nothing but my beautiful baby girl. I love her so much. I loved her enough to leave her. I could not offer her nothing but now I can. It took me five years to get my life together and when I came back for my baby, she was gone. Deidra needs her Mother. Do you hear me Jay, she needs me and not you. Let her go. You need to let her go." That said, she walked away.

Verna touched Jay's arm. "Come on, let's go get some lunch. No need to hang around here for an hour."

Jay snatched his arm away. "I don't want any lunch. I am about to lose my only family."

"I am your family," Verna said. "And besides, we have not lost Dee yet."

"You heard what the Judge said. Dee is as good as gone. If only I had not sent her out that day she would still be mine."

"She will always be yours Jay. No one can take that away from you."

Jay yelled. "You don't know how I feel!"

Verna was hurt. She thought about her sister and how it hurt so much not to be with her. "I do know Jay more than you or anyone will ever know."

Jay saw the hurt in Verna's eyes. "I'm sorry baby. I'm so sorry. I did not mean it. I am so upset right now. I know it hurts you too to see Dee taken away. Let's go get some lunch."

When they returned to court everyone was already inside the courtroom.

The Judge addressed Jay. "Young man do you think you can contain yourself. If you can not you will be charged with contempt of court. Do you understand?"

"I understand," Jay said.

"Will all parties approach the bench," the Judge said.

As they all stood at the bench, Dee held Jay's hand. Jay noticed that her hand was shaking.

The Judge spoke. "My decision is as followed. Deidra Wilson will be released and placed in the permanent custody of her Mother, Mrs. Camille Baker." The conditions being that the child is placed in a drug treatment program. She is to be immediately assessed and enrolled in school. The family is ordered to attend family counseling. The case will be transferred to Virginia and Ordered to come before that state court in one year for a Review Hearing."

The Judge looked at Jay. "Do you wish to appeal the decision of this court, Mr. Wilson?"

Jay thought about what Dee's Mother said. If you love her let her go. It hurt him, but he knew she was right. He had to do this one thing for Dee. He had to let her go. "No, I do not wish to appeal."

Dee started crying. "I don't want to go."

"Can I talk to her for a few minutes," Jay asked?

"No," the Caseworker said. "I don't feel that it is in the best interest of the child to," Dee's Mother interrupted the Caseworker.

"Give him five minutes, Mrs. Ward."

"Only five minutes," Mrs. Ward replied.

Jay took Dee's hand. "Listen Dee you are strong. Don't cry do you hear me?"

"I'm afraid," Dee said.

"I have never heard you say you are afraid before."

"I don't want to leave you, Jay."

"I will be with you always."

"No," Dee said.

"Have I ever lied to you, Dee?"

"No," Dee said.

"Go with your Mother. Do what I tell you."

Dee slowly walked to her Mother. Jay took Verna's hand and they slowly walked out. He did not look back. There were tears in his eyes. He did not want Dee to see him cry.

When Verna and Jay returned home, they sat in silence. As Jay thought of Dee, Verna was reminded of the lost of her Joy.

"Where's the weed," Jay asked?

"There is no more," Verna said. "All we have is the crack."

"Well, break up one of those rocks and roll some up in a cigarette."

Verna wanted to protest but she did not. She crushed some up in a cigarette. Together they smoked in silence.

JOY

Joy could not believe it was graduation day. Sam and Mama Mae were so proud of her. She had graduated with honor in the top 5% of her class. She had received a full scholarship to a University in Atlanta Georgia. She hated the thought of leaving Mama Mae and Sam. They encouraged her to go. This is what they had dreamed for Joy. Mama Mae reminded her that she would be home for holidays. She also reminded Joy of her dream that Joy would one day be someone important and special. Sam told Joy when Mama Mae dreams watch out. Joy only wished Verna could be there to see her graduate. I did it Verna, she thought.

After graduation, Sam and Mama Mae took Joy to an expensive seafood restaurant.

"I don't know what to order," Joy said. "It all looks so good and expensive."

"Don't worry about the price," Mama Mae said. "You get what you want, child."

Joy ordered a seafood platter consisting of shrimp scampi, scallops, and flounder stuffed with crab meat dressing. Sam ordered a bottle of champagne. "A toast to our baby."

Joy had never drank wine before. She sipped a little from her glass. "Umm, this is good. Try some Mama Mae."

"Oh no," Mama Mae looked shocked.

"Oh come on," Sam said. "a little wine won't hurt ya."

"You know I am a Christian woman."

"I believe in the word," Sam said, "but I don't believe the Lord would burn a soul in hell for drinking a little wine."

Mama Mae looked at Sam. "I tell you what, I don't want to find out. You let me know when you get there."

Joy laughed.

Sam called the waiter to the table. "Can you please exchange this wine for some good sparkling cider?"

They all laughed. After dinner they ordered peach cobbler. They ate in silence each thinking their own thoughts. Joy was thinking about how much she wished Verna was here to share her special day with her special family.

"Well," Mae said. "I have to admit that was mighty tasty pie, but I still believe mine got it beat. What yall say?"

Sam rubbed his head. "I don't know it sure is close."

"Hush your mouth," Mae said. "What you think Joy?"

"Mama Mae this might be good, but your pie is cooked with love and this pie can't touch yours."

"Now that's my baby," Mama Mae said affectionately.

Sam touched Joy's hand. "We have something special for you."

Mama Mae reached into her old brown purse. She pulled out a small box. "Open up baby."

"You didn't have to do this," Joy said. "You both have done too much for me already. Mama Mae if you had not taken me in, Lord knows where I would be now. You and Sam taught me that I am not a bad person. You taught me how to love myself."

"You bought us so much Joy," Sam said. "We want to give some back."

Joy smiled. "The school ring you bought me was enough."

Mae looked exasperated. "Child if you don't hush your mouth and open that box. I ain't never whipped your butt but you gonna get one."

Joy laughed, opening the box. She pulled out a set of keys. She looked at them stunned.

Sam was smiling. "Look at that child. She in shock."

"Let's go out and look at your car," Mama Mae said.

Joy could not believe how blessed she was. She never knew life could be so wonderful.

"It's in the parking lot," Sam said. "I drove it up here earlier then caught the bus back home."

"I can't believe this," Joy said. "I am so happy."

"It's used but it's a nice car."

"I don't care if it is on one wheel. I love it already because it is from you and Mama Mae."

"Get in," Sam said. "It even has a radio and air condition."

"Well," Mama Mae said. "Don't just stand there with your mouth hangin all open get in and give us old folks a ride home."

For Joy the summer went fast. She volunteered to work at a drug rehabilitation center. She was so touched by these people. They had so much pain. She somehow knew that this was her calling to help these people. Some of them had been abused physically, sexually, and mentally. These people responded to her very well. She used her own personal testimony of sexual abuse and the lost of her sister as a way to let them know that she too knew what hurt and pain felt like and that she really cared for them. It did not take long before Joy became known at the center as the best counselor there. Joy worked best with teenagers. Somehow they kept coming back. She seemed much older than her eighteen years. She was so effective that the Director of the program decided to hire her part time. She did not make much money, but the feeling that she was helping someone was worth more than any amount of money she could earn.

It came time for Joy to go to college. The Rehabilitation Center gave her a party. They presented her with a collection of one thousand dollars as well as gifts that she would need for college. All the youth in the program were invited. They were sad to see her go. The Director presented her with a certificate recognizing her for outstanding guidance in a rehabilitative setting.

The Director said, "You have been an outstanding influence and great asset to this program. I wish you great success and extend an offer for you to continue to work with the program during your summer vacations. You will always have a position with the center and may God bless you in all you do."

"Thank You," Joy said. "I just want to say to everyone in this program I will miss you. Many of you have come to me to tell me that you have found strength in me and now that I am leaving you feel lost. You are not lost sisters and brothers. The strength you felt was your own strength. I only helped you find the strength that God had already placed there. Now that you have claimed your strength, use it. When you are out on the streets and you feel the urge to use drugs or alcohol, I want you to call on that strength. I want to tell you that sometimes it may seem like it is

gone, but remember my friends, it is never gone. No one can take
from you what God has given you. Sometimes I have to call on
that strength to make it. Remember you have strength. I know it is
there in you because I have seen it. I have felt it and so have you
so grab on to it and don't let go. If you need help, continue to seek
help and remember use your strength and I love you."

Joy looked around at all the faces. She was touched deeply. What
she saw was hope in the eyes of those who were hopeless. She
knew more than ever, this was her calling.

University life was great. Joy majored in counseling. Since she
had a full scholarship, she did not have to pay for room, board,
tuition, or her books. In spite of this, Joy chose to work. The
Director from the center in Detroit had arranged a part time job
for Joy at a drug counseling center in Atlanta. Joy quickly became
well known. People would come in from off the streets and ask
for her by name. Near the end of Joy's first year of college, the
university's paper had done an article about Joy and her
outstanding work as a counselor. Joy sent a copy of the article to
Mama Mae and Sam. Joy was so busy, she did not have much

time to talk to them, but they knew that she loved them very much.

During Joy's second year of college, she continued to work at the Center in Atlanta. However, she was not satisfied. She felt she was not doing enough. The people coming into the Center were not the ones who needed it the most. The ones who needed it the most were still out there on the streets. She felt an urgency to reach those persons. Joy went to the Director.

"Ms. Lewis, there is a problem with this program."

"What is the problem?"

"We are not reaching enough people."

"We can only reach those who come in for help," Ms. Lewis said.

"I have an idea," Joy continued. "I need your permission to start my own program. I will need as many staff as you can provide."

"What is your idea," Ms. Lewis asked?

"My idea is very basic. If we can't get the people in for counseling, then we take the counseling to the people."

"Am I hearing you right," Ms. Lewis asked.

"Exactly," Joy said. "I want to take the program to the streets. I want to talk to the addicts right on the street corner."

"It all sounds good but it is too dangerous. I will never be able to get the city to approve it."

"All I am asking for you to do is try and I will do the rest."

"O.k., I will give it a try. Put your proposal on paper for me. I will call the City Director as soon as your written proposal is ready."

Joy handed Ms. Lewis a typed proposal. Ms. Lewis was impressed. "You are proficient."

After two months of trying to get Joy's proposal approved, Ms. Lewis somehow managed to get the go ahead to proceed. She called Joy into the office. "The only stipulation is that you have to sign an agreement not holding the city liable for any injuries including death that may occur on the job. I am sorry but that is the only way I could get the city to approve this project."

Joy smiled. "Good enough. What about staff?"

"They only allotted enough money for two staff members other than yourself."

"I guess that will have to do. Can I pick my own staff?"

"I don't see why not as long as they sign the agreement."

"When can I begin?"

"Since the money has already been allotted, as soon as you get your staff together, you can begin."

Joy was so excited. "I guess it is time for me to get busy. Thank you Ms. Lewis. I know this can work."

"I hope so because I put myself on the spot."

"You won't be disappointed."

Ms. Lewis stood to shake Joy's hand. "I don't think I will be disappointed."

Joy caused a big stir in the city by picking as her staff two prior drug addicts who had come to the center for help. No one seemed to think it would work. At first, there was little response to the program. The city threatened to cancel the funds for the program. Joy knew the problem was she needed to spend more time on the streets. She had to make an important decision. She called Mama Mae and told her what she wanted to do. "Joy," Mama Mae said. "I will stand behind your decision." The next day Joy quit school. Joy and her staff began to spend most of their time on the streets. She rented a room from Ms. Lewis. Most of the time, she was not in her room, but on the streets. After three months of practically living on the streets, Joy began to see a change. The people were responding to Joy and her staff. They realized that this young woman really cared for them. They saw her and her staff out on the streets everyday. The Center was packed. Joy was bringing more and more people in everyday who wanted help. The success of this program quickly spread throughout the state. Joy was getting offers to help start similar programs in other areas of the state. She began to speak to large groups. Joy concentrated on Elementary and Middle schools. She knew it was very important to stop the problem before it began. Joy began making good money from her speaking engagements, but the best satisfaction came from knowing that she was helping someone.

At the beginning of the next fiscal year, the city was so impressed by the success of Joy's program. They asked her to head her own separate program. She was given her own headquarters and a staff of 20. She was given a large salary. Joy was speechless. In addition to her salary she was bringing in half the amount of her salary in speeches alone. Joy accepted the offer. She called Mama Mae and told her all that had happened.

Mama Mae said, "I am so proud of you. I knew you could do it."

Joy had something else on her mind. "I want you and Sam to come live with me. I can buy a nice home for us."

Joy heard Mama Mae sigh. "I know you can Joy, but I'm an old settled woman. This here is my home. This old house ain't much but it has many memories. I can't leave now, honey."

Joy was disappointed but she really understood. "I understand. It was the first real home I ever knew and it means a great deal to me too. At least let me fix it up for you."

"Baby, it is fine the way it is."

Joy was stern. "Let me do this one thing for you, Mama Mae."

"Baby, I see you aint giving up. If you want to spend your money on an old woman, then so be it."

Joy laughed. "Tell Sam I love him and if he can't come live with me, then he will be getting his home redecorated also."

Mae laughed. "Now what that old fool gonna do with a redecorated home?"

Joy's popularity continued to grow. She began to travel from state to state on speaking engagements. She also trained other agencies across the nation in starting their own outreach programs.

Joy was able to afford a luxury penthouse apartment overlooking a private lake. She would send for Mama Mae and Sam frequently. Together they would spend a day at the lake fishing and talking. Joy had not forgotten Verna. Now that she had money, she was able to hire a private investigator to look for Verna. Sam asked. "Why you still looking for your sister? Let it go before you find out something you don't want to know."

Joy sighed. The thought of Verna still made her sad. "Please understand. Whether good or bad, I have to find out what happened to her. Not knowing eats me up inside. If I have to go to my grave trying to find out what happened to her, then I will. If I have to spend every dime I have to find her, then I will. I can never stop searching for her, never."

Joy looked at Mama Mae. "Do you remember when you were sick and you had that dream? You said I would be somebody. You also said that I would see my sister again."

"I remember," Mama Mae said.

"Do you believe what you said?"

"Why yes child, you know that I believe."

"Me too," Joy said. "I have to believe. Part of your dream came true. I am very successful and I know that one day I will see Verna again."

"Hang in there child, Mama Mae said. "You will see your sister again. Trust me."

VERNA

Jay had become more distant. He became caught up in selling
crack. It seemed the only thing he and Verna did together was
smoke crack. He never mentioned Dee. One day Verna asked him
about his Mother. He told her his Mother was never around for
him. He could remember as a small child being left alone in a
small filthy apartment with no food to eat until one day his
Grandmother came and got him and took him to live with her. He
remembers his Mother dropping by from time to time. He also
remembered violent arguments between his Mother and
Grandmother. He said one day his Grandmother told him his
Mother was never coming back. He was five at the time. He did

not learn until he was nine years old that his Mother had died on the streets of a heroin overdose. He never went to a funeral and to this day, he does not know where his Mother is buried. Jay showed no emotions in talking about his Mother. When Verna asked him did he want to know where his Mother was laid to rest? Jay just looked at her with a blank look and asked what for?

Over the next year, Jay and Verna spent most of their time selling crack. They did not make much money because whatever they made went back into supporting their own crack habit. Sometimes they would sit around for days at a time hitting the pipe. She did not even want to have sex with Jay. This did not seem to bother Jay because he never touched her anymore. Verna had lost over twenty pounds off of her already thin frame. One day Verna and Jay were sitting around smoking crack. Verna was sitting around in her underwear as she sometimes did when they were alone. They became aware of a knock at the door.

"Who is it," Jay asked?

"I want to buy a rock," a voice answered through the door.

"What size," Jay asked?

"Just a fifty dollar piece," the voice replied.

"O.k.," Jay said. "But me and my woman chillin in here. Slip the money under the door. After I get the cash, I will crack the door and hand you the rock, man."

A fifty dollar bill slipped under the door.

As Jay cracked open the door to hand the voice his purchase, four white men burst through the door. Verna screamed and tried to cover herself.

"Yo man, what's up like this," Jay yelled. He was caught off guard.

"Police," one of them shouted as he flung Jay to the floor and handcuffed him behind his back. Verna tried to run to the back bedroom but one of the cops grabbed her by the arm.

Jay struggled. "Man, leave my woman alone. She doesn't have nothing to do with this. It's me you want, man."

"I just want to cover myself," Verna cried.

"It won't be any need for that." He said grinning.

"Leave her alone." Jay struggled on the floor.

"Shut up nigger." An older white cop said as he kicked Jay in the stomach.

"You dirty white racist pig. Take these cuffs off me," Jay yelled in anger.

The cop who was holding Verna started to laugh. "Take the cuffs off him. Let's see what the boy can do. Do you think you can take all of us, boy?" The cop was amused.

Verna was screaming. "Leave him alone!"

"Maybe not," Jay said. "But you will be the first pig I am coming after, believe that!"

The smile on the cop's face vanished. His face turned red.

"Why you," he said as he approached Jay. He was about to lift Jay off the floor when three vice detectives came in the apartment.

"Vice squad," one of them said. "We will take over from here."

Verna was screaming.

Jay was crying tears of anger.

"What's going on here," a vice officer asked? It was obvious he had rank because the cops all seemed to straighten up.

"Nothing," the cop holding Verna said.

"Well it sure looks like something is going on here. Someone get the young lady a shirt."

The cop holding Verna escorted her to the bedroom. "Get dressed," he ordered giving her a shove.

Jay was on the floor spitting up blood. "What's wrong with him," the vice officer asked?

"He just had a little accident," one of the cops responded.

"Get this place searched," the vice officer ordered. Take these young people to the station and book them. I better not see a scratch on them when I get down to the station."

When Jay and Verna arrived at the station they were separated.

"You don't know nothing," Jay yelled to Verna. "I am not going to let you go down for this. Do you hear me?"

"I love you," Verna yelled back as a white female officer led her down the hall. Verna was taken into a small room by the white female officer and a black female officer who had joined her.

"Take all your clothes off," the white officer said.

"Why," Verna asked a little frightened.

"Look," the black female cop said. "Either you cooperate and take your clothes off or we will take them off for you."

Verna was humiliated. She slowly took her clothes off. A nurse came in and began to strap Verna's legs to a table.

"Relax honey," she said. "This won't hurt."

Verna was crying. "What are you going to do?"

"A body cavity search."

Verna was confused. "What's that?"

"It's just an examination of your vaginal and anal cavities. If you relax then it will be less uncomfortable for you."

"Why are you doing this to me?"

"It's procedure whenever there is any kind of drug charges involved. You would be surprised at what kind of goodies we have found during these examinations."

Verna watched as the nurse put gloves on. She closed her eyes tight as the nurse approached her. Regardless of how tight she closed her eyes, she could not block out the humiliation of those probing fingers in her vagina. Once the examination was completed, they made Verna take a shower and wash her hair with special shampoo and soap designed to kill head and body lice. It smelled awful.

"I don't have lice," Verna protested.

"Honey we don't know what you got."

Once the shower was completed they took Verna to an area where she got her picture taken and they also fingerprinted her. They asked her if she would like to make her phone call.

"No, I don't have anyone to call," she said sadly.

They took Verna to a small cell with four bunks in it.

"We will be back to question you after we finish with your boyfriend," the Officer said.

Verna was afraid. She had heard horror stories about life in jail. She thought back to times when she and Sue had sat around and discussed what they thought prison was like. It seemed like a life time ago when she and Sue would hang out and have a good time. Now Sue was dead. Joy was gone. Dee was gone. She may never see Jay again and she was locked up. She sat down on the only empty bunk and hung her head in her hands.

Someone near her spoke. "Hang in their sister."

Verna did not know who had spoken to her. She looked up to see who she shared the cell with. She saw three other black girls in the cell. She wondered if this was intentional. She thought segregation was in the past. She remembered how the white cops had treated her and Jay.

"What's your name one of the girls asked?"

"Verna."

"I am Rose. What they holding you for?"

"I think possession of cocaine."

"Oh no, not a drug charge. This state is hard on drug offenses. Speaking of drugs, you don't look too well, sister. As the old folks used to say, you look like you got a pretty strong monkey riding your back."

Verna became defensive. "I don't have a drug problem."

Rose continued. "Oh still in the denial stage I see. You will see when you have to go without it for a while."

Verna was insulted. "Of course I get high every now and then but don't everybody?"

"You don't have to convince me," Rose said. "I had a pretty strong habit myself, but prison life makes you shake it at least for a while unless you can come up with the dollars to get a hit. I have been down three times."

"What they holding you for," Verna asked?

"Parole violation and maybe an assault charge. All of us will go up before the Judge tomorrow. We will probably get shipped by the end of the month. Depending on whether or not you go to trial or plea out. If you lucky you will get to do your time here because State prison ain't no joke."

"Amen," the other girls in the cell echoed.

"How much dope you have on you," Rose asked?

"I don't know. My boyfriend kept tabs on that. I don't even know how much we had in the apartment."

"They got your boyfriend too, huh."

"Yeah," Verna said.

"He won't cop out on you will he," one of the other girls asked.

"Never," Verna said. "He told me he wouldn't let me fall for this."

"Yeah, I heard that before. By the way, my name is Crystal. My old man told me the same thing. Here I am still locked up and his black butt out there walking the streets."

"Yeah," Rose agreed. "Brothers ain't about nothing. When the stink hits the fan they leave you all alone."

Verna sat in silence. Not my Jay, she thought. He would never do that to me.

An officer came up. "Verna, come with me."

"Be strong sister," Rose said. "Don't let them see you sweat."

"Amen," the other girls echoed.

They took Verna into a small room with no windows. There was only a small table and three chairs. On the table sat a tape recorder and some paper and a pen. The same Vice Detectives were present. Also present was the black female cop who had been nasty to her earlier and two other people who Verna did not recognize. The Vice Detective who had done all the talking in the apartment spoke. "Verna Edwards, I believe you have been read your rights."

Verna remained silent.

"Is that correct," he asked?

"Yeah," Verna said without looking at him.

He turned to the female cop. "Just to be safe read them again."

"Sit down," the female cop said.

As Verna sat down she was read her rights. The words did not mean a thing to her. Verna looked from one officer to another. She was very paranoid. She wished she could have one hit to calm her nerves. The crack that she and Jay had smoked earlier had worn off. She could only think about getting out and finding some dope.

They began to ask Verna questions. Her head jerked from one officer to the next. They are all out to get me, she thought.

The female cop spoke. "She is a dope fiend. You won't be able to get anything out of her."

"I agree," the Vice Detective said. The only thing on her mind is crack. She is pitiful."

At the mention of crack, Verna lifted her head.

"Crack," Verna whispered. "Where it at?" "Where it at, Mister?"

"Cut the tape recorder off," the Vice Detective said.

"If you talk to us we will get you some," he said.

"Where it at," Verna asked again?

"Will you talk," he asked her?

"Yeah, where it at?"

"Turn the tape recorder back on," he ordered. "She's ready to talk."

"Tell us about your boyfriend," he asked. "We know he's been selling crack. Is that right?"

"Don't know nothing," Verna said.

"Where it at," she asked again.

The vice detective decided to try a different approach. "You know your boyfriend told us it was your dope. Now why don't you tell us whose dope it was?"

"No," Verna said. "Don't know nothing. Verna dropped her head," Where it at?"

The vice detective shook his head pathetically. "We are not going to get much out of her. Anyway we got enough on the boyfriend for felony possession with intent to distribute. Looks like the most we are going to get on her is a simple possession charge. That should be enough to get her a couple of years in prison. Dry her out a little bit."

They took Verna back to her cell. She was told she would go before the Judge in the morning. Verna lay on her bunk. "Where it at?"

"Where what at," Crystal asked?

"Don't you know she is having some serious cravings," Rose said. "Best thing to do is to let her sweat it out. She will be better in the morning."

Verna moaned all night. The next morning she awoke feeling very
bad.

"Well, look who decided to join the land of the living," Rose said.

"How are you doing sugar," Crystal asked?

Crystal was an average looking woman of about twenty-six years
old. She was brown skinned. She had medium length hair and a
wide nose and mouth.

"How you think she doing," Man said. Man was a tall dark skin
woman in her early twenties. She looked more like a man than a
woman. She had two gold teeth. She wore a very short afro. From
her ear dangled one gold earring. When she spoke her voice was
deep. "I didn't introduce myself last night. Just call me man like
everyone else does. I like it."

Verna vaguely remembered her from the night before. She did not
remember much of the night before.

"What happened last night?" She asked no one in particular.

"Honey, you moaned all night long," Crystal said. "You were
asking for someone named Jay and Joy. Now we figured Jay must
be your boyfriend, but who is this Joy chick?"

"Joy is my baby sister. I have not seen her in years. I don't even know where she is."

"Why," Rose asked?

Verna related how her and Joy became separated.

"That's deep," Rose said.

"Yeah," Crystal added. "We all are going to court today. We will all probably be sent to State Prison. Let's make a pack to look out for each other."

"I'm down with that," Rose said. "How about you Man?"

"You got it baby."

All eyes turned to Verna. "I'm in," she said.

For breakfast they were given grits or cold cereal, apple juice and dry toast.

"Where the butter and jam at," Rose asked the guard?

"In your mind," the guard responded.

"Dog," rose yelled after her. "I'll see you when I get out."

At 9:00a.m., the guard came back. "Verna Edwards come with me."

"Be strong sister," Rose said.

"Right on," Man added.

"Thanks," Verna said. However, she knew that she would not be strong. She had already started to shake and sweat. "I wish I had just one hit." Suddenly a huge amount of shame overcame her. A nobody she said to herself. Just a nobody junkie.

"Young lady," the Judge said. "You have been charged with simple possession of crack cocaine. Have you been provided with a court appointed public defender?"

"No sir," Verna said.

"Why haven't she been provided a public defender," the Judge demanded. This case is at recess. Bailiff see to it that she has ample time with a court appointed attorney. Bring in the next defendant."

As Verna was led out, Man was being brought into the court room. She gave Verna the peace sign. Verna was brought into a room with a long table with about ten chairs on each side.

"Have a seat," a distinguished looking white man said.

Verna sat on one side of the table.

"I am Attorney Craig. I have been appointed as your Attorney. I have reviewed the charges against you. For what I can see your best bet is to plead guilty as charged. The bad news is you will probably get between one to three years at State. But the good news is that with good time and because it is your first offense you will probably be out in less than half that time." He did not give Verna time to respond. Nor did he ask her what happened. "Come on," he said standing up. "I will do what I can for you. Just plead guilty."

Verna was confused. She was ignorant about the legal system. She just wanted to get it over with. When Verna returned to the court room, Man was being dragged out by two Deputy Sheriff. Man was very angry and cursing loudly. Man was so mad she did not see Verna being led in.

"Young lady please stand," the Judge said. "Have you had time to consult with your Attorney?"

The Attorney answered for Verna. "Yes she has, Your Honor."

"How do you plead," the Judge asked?

Verna said nothing. The Judge was frustrated. He asked the Attorney, "How does your client plea?"

"My client respectfully enters a plea of guilty as charged."

The Judge spoke. "Let the records indicate that the defendant,
Verna Edwards, has entered a plea of guilty for possession of
crack cocaine. Now does the defendant or her legal representative
wish to address the court before sentencing?"

Verna's Attorney spoke up. "Your Honor, I would like to point
out to the court that my client is a first time offender and quite
clearly a junkie. I would like to recommend that a drug
rehabilitation center would be most appropriate for my offender,
instead of incarceration. She would receive the treatment that she
needs for her drug addiction."

"I will take that into consideration," the Judge replied. "Court will
be adjourned for one hour."

Verna was placed in a holding cell for one hour. She continued to
stare in space. Verna was led back into the court room. She was in
handcuffs and leg shackles. She had on an orange jump suit and
flip flops on her feet.

The Judge entered and they were all instructed to rise.

"You may be seated," the Judge said. Everyone sat as instructed.
The Judge sat in silence for five minutes which seemed like hours
to Verna. He looked up. "Ms. Verna Edwards please stand. I have

taken into consideration that this is your first offense and that you are a drug addict. I do feel that you should be placed in a residential drug rehabilitation center rather than prison. Regrettably, there is no room at any of the residential treatment programs. As a society with rules and regulations we can not let this crime go unpunished. In sentencing I have opted to give you the minimum sentence since you are a first time offender. Ms. Edwards I sentence you to one year at Women's State Prison. I only hope that you will seek the help you need. Court is adjourned."

Verna was led back to her cell. Her cell mates were sitting around. Everyone seemed to be in a depressed mood.

"What you get baby," Man asked?

"One year," Verna said sadly.

"Dang, you lucked up," Rose said. "They stuck it to us. We are getting shipped Friday. They ain't wasting no time."

"Yeah three days from now," Crystal said. "When you leaving?"

"I don't know," Verna answered.

"You will probably get shipped with us. I heard an officer say everyone sentenced today will be shipped Friday."

"I'm afraid," Verna said. "What's it like?"

Man looked at Verna. "I've been down twice and it aint so bad."

"Yeah," Crystal said that is because no one is going to mess with your mannish behind."

"No one is gonna mess with ya'll either. Remember our pack, Man stressed."

"Pack or not," Rose cut in, "nobody gonna mess with me. You stick with me Verna you will be straight."

"Yeah I got your back," Man said.

Crystal added. "You are fresh meat. They are going to try you, believe that. They tried me the first time I went down but I quickly checked that junk."

"You didn't check nothing," Rose said. "All you did was found you a lesbian to protect you."

"Now wait a minute," Crystal said. "I don't go that way."

Rose laughed. "Yeah, I guess you forgot I was down the same time as you and that lesbian Pat led you around like a lost puppy. She probably still up there." Rose was cracking up.

Crystal tried to change the subject. "Anyway, we arc all going to look out for each other."

Man was not going to let Crystal off so easy. "Don't worry Crystal. I will claim you as my woman. Pat won't mess with you. I am going to have a string of women running behind me."

"Forget ya'll," Crystal said.

"O.k., Rose said. We are going to leave Crystal alone. We all agree to stick together."

Man would not let it go. She was having too much fun. "Why you sticking up for Crystal? You and her got it going on?"

Rose quickly responded. "Now you know better than that. I love me some men and that thing between their legs. Big, little, red, yellow, black or white. Just give it to me." Verna found herself laughing for the first time.

"Look ya'll," Crystal said. Verna is laughing.

Man asked Verna, "What about you? Do you get into women?"

"No, no, no," Verna said laughing. "I am saving all my love for my man. We have been through a lot. It has made us even closer."

"I heard that," Crystal said.

"I wish I could find out how he is doing," Verna said sadly.

"Leave it to me," Rose said.

When the guard came with lunch, Rose approached the bars. She slipped the guard a bill. "Why don't you pass a note to the men's side for me?"

"It will cost you another bill," the officer said.

"Dang," Rose said. "It only used to cost one bill."

"Inflation," the guard replied.

Verna wrote Jay about what happened in court and told him where she was going. She told him she loved him. She also told him she did not tell the pigs anything.

"Do you think he will get it," Verna asked Rose?

"Yeah, lesson number one, there is nothing that can not be bought. Money is very valuable in this game if you can find a way to sneak it in."

Verna said. "I don't have any money. I guess I owe you."

Man cut in. "Lesson number two is never owe anybody nothing."

"That's right," Rose said. "For the record you don't owe me jack."

The same guard returned an hour later to pick up their lunch trays.

"That sure is a fine looking man you have," she said handing Verna a note. "He was very relieved to receive your note."

127

"Thank You," Verna said.

"No sweat. If you got the dime I got the time."

Verna's hand trembled. Enclosed was a fifty dollar bill and a note that read, hang in there, Verna. It is good that you only got one year. You will be out in no time. Make sure you stay out of trouble and get all your good time. I am sorry I got you involved. I was not so lucky. I got seven years at the penitentiary, a rough place. The prosecutors wanted to give me twenty years like I killed someone. I heard they stick it to you for selling crack which is almost double the time given for selling powder cocaine. Now you tell me what the difference is. Crack is just some powder cooked up. I tell you it is a black thing and you know it. Anyway my Public Defender was good enough to get me a seven year plea because of my clean record. The good news is that if I keep a good record in prison with good time I can be out in four years but the bad news is that it is almost impossible to keep a clean record in the penitentiary. Baby, with me being young and fine, I will have to prove myself, so just look for me to do the seven years. Part of me want to tell you to do your time and get out and forget you ever knew me. The other part wants me to tell you to come see me when you get out. I know the thought of you waiting for me will help me make it. Pretty lady, I do love you. Sitting here I have been thinking. I have done two very wrong things in my life. I messed up Dee's life and I messed up yours. I have done one right thing and that was to let Dee go. So now I must do the other right thing and tell you to forget about me. So you hang in there my pretty lady. Love, Jay.

I will never leave you Jay, Verna thought.

"He got seven years," Verna said.

"That's not too bad," Rose said. "With the charges he had. He could have gotten fifteen to twenty easily. It must have been his first offense."

"It was," Verna said.

Friday came. Verna was even more frightened than when she left home with nowhere to go years ago.

"Chill out," Man said. "You got fear written all over your face."

"Yeah," Rose said. "You don't want to let them women know you are afraid."

The same guard who had passed the notes came to the cell. "O.k. girls, we will be leaving out in about thirty minutes, be ready."

Verna addressed the guard. "Can you arrange for me to see my boyfriend before I leave?"

"I'm sorry," she said. "That's risking my job too much. That would cost at least several hundred dollars, but I can tell him a message for you."

"Tell him I will always wait for him."

"I will tell him."

The bus ride was silent. There were twenty women on the bus. Everyone was lost in their own thoughts. The bus pulled up into a large brick building that looked like it was two hundred years old. They entered through two electronic gates. Verna would never forget the loud sounds the gates made as they closed and locked.

"Hang in there, sister," Rose said.

"I feel like an animal, Rose."

"While you are in here, you are an animal," Rose responded.

They were taken to a part of the building that opened up into a long hallway. On both sides of the hallway were twenty steel doors on each side. These steel doors opened up into very small living areas which included a small wired bunk bed with a very thin mattress, a toilet and a sink. There was hardly any room to walk around.

"Listen up!" A female Correctional Officer ordered. "For some of you this is all new. But, I see quite a few familiar faces. For the new ones welcome to quarantine hall. As a new inmate you will spend a total of twenty one days on quarantine hall. After twenty one days you will be assigned and moved to your permanent living assignments. On quarantine hall you will go through the orientation process. We will assign you your permanent inmate number which will be how we see you from that point on as a number. We will tell you about institutional rules and regulations. We will test you in order to place you as far as school is concerned. During this time you will be sent to the institution classification committee whereas you will be assigned a custody level which will determine your level of freedom. This level determines if you will be allowed to go to school, recreation, chow hall, activities and so on or if you will be detained within your building. The lower the custody level the more privileges. So when I call your name you will be assigned a number and a cell."

"What's up Officer Kelly," Rose said?

"I see you are back again," the officer said.

"Yeah, I could not stay away. Can you hook me and my home girl, Verna, up in the same room? She is new and it is only for twenty one days?"

Rose and Verna were assigned the same room. There were only two assigned to each small room. Crystal was assigned a room with a girl named Gail who she knew from being down before. Man was placed in a room with a first timer. She was very happy about this.

"We will pass out blankets and other personal items after lunch," Officer Kelly said.

The end of the hall opened up into a large recreation room which also served as the dining area for that hall. For twenty one days, they were not to have any contact with the general population. Their meals would be brought to the unit. After the twenty one days they would be allowed to take their meals at the central mess hall with the rest of the general population.

Verna heard a loud piercing whistled. She jumped.

"Relax," Rose said. "You will get used to this. That whistle means it is lunch time. The Whistle will tell you when to eat, when to get up, when to go to sleep, and when to get counted."

"I am not hungry," Verna said.

Rose shook her head. "Come on Verna. Get with the program. You can't stay shut up forever. If you don't go out the women will think you are scared and on the real, a punk. If they think you are scared, they will give you a hard time."

"I am scared," Verna said.

"Do you want a hard time," Rose asked?

"No, I don't want a hard time. I have had too many hard times as it is."

"O.k.," Rose said. "The food here is much better than in the city jail."

Verna reluctantly stepped on the hall with Rose. She was amazed at all the women now on the hall and how loud it had become.

"Everyone comes out to eat," Rose explained.

Crystal and her roommate Gail saved Rose and Verna a seat at the table. Man was sitting with her new roommate. She winked as Rose and Verna walked by.

"That crazy Man is at it already," Rose commented.

The food was much better than jail. They had chili Mac, rolls, green beans, and fruit cocktail. To drink there was ice tea and milk.

Rose addressed Verna. "After the kitchen crew cleans up, we will have half an hour before the afternoon count to socialize. After count, we will be locked in our rooms until dinner. After dinner we will have free time until sundown count which is usually around 8:30p.m. After sundown count, we are locked in our rooms until the next morning. When we leave quarantine hall, the routine will change and we won't be locked down as much."

"Yeah," Crystal added. I am looking forward to getting off quarantine hall and moving on to population. I am ready to go out on the ball field for recreation instead of being locked down all day and night."

Twenty one days passed quickly for Verna. She was assigned to school and although she never completed 11th grade, her scores were high enough to place her in the 12th grade as a senior. Her work assignment was the laundry. She was placed on hall six.

Man and Crystal were placed on the same hall as her, but Rose was placed on a different hall. Verna was very lonely. Man was busy chasing women and Crystal had met up with some girls from her neighborhood. She kept to herself. No one bothered Verna because true to her word, Man had put the word out that nobody better not even think to mess with Verna. Verna hardly ever saw Rose except in passing to school or work. She was miserable. She wished she could write Jay. Unfortunately, there was a rule that no one could write anyone else in the system unless they were immediate family and that had to be approved. Five months passed and Verna would be going up for parole in a month. She did not know what she would do or where she would even go. What she did know is that she wanted out of here.

One day Verna was sitting in the recreation area watching Good Times when three white girls came and changed the channel to All in the Family.

"I was watching that," Verna said.

"Too bad," the leader said. "You the only one want to watch it. It's three of us and majority rules."

"First come, first serve," Verna replied.

"Not on this hall," the leader said.

Verna checked them out. The leader was an obvious butch. She was built like a man and even had a mustache. I don't want to mess with her, Verna thought. The other two girls drew their boldness from the butch. Verna had been down long enough to know that she had to stand up to these girls and not be punked. She stood up and turned the television back to Good Times. The three girls surrounded her. "We ain't watching no nigger show," the leader said.

Verna prayed that the guard would come. They were never around when they were needed. A crowd had begun to develop.

Now that she had a crowd, the butch pushed Verna.

Verna hit the floor. She stood up and swung with her eyes closed. She had never been in a fight before. She missed the butch. The crowd of women laughed. The butch pushed Verna again.

"What's going on over here," a voice said.

All eyes turned to see Man break through the crowd. Crystal and two other black girls were following behind Man.

"Oh No," Man said I know you ho's ain't messing with my home girl."

"And what if we are," the butch said.

"You know I got your back," Crystal said as she stepped up.

"Ain't nobody messing with Verna."

"What's the deal," man asked Verna.

Verna told Man what happened.

"Oh Yeah," Man said looking at the butch. "You better back down."

Everyone on the hall was afraid of Man. The butch started walking away.

"Nigger," she mumbled under her breath.

Man reached out and punched her straight in her mouth. Blood and teeth were falling out of her mouth. That was Crystal's cue. She grabbed one of the other girls and went to work.

The next thing Verna knew people were fighting all over the place. She was blindly swinging in the air. The officer came out of her office. She blew her whistle, but no one responded.

"10-33," she yelled in her radio in a panic. 10-33 was the code for need help quickly. Uniforms came from everywhere and started snatching people up. Verna felt herself being lifted up and carried away. The next thing she knew she was down in a cell in the basement better known as segregation unit or the hole.

"Hey yo!" Man yelled from the next cell. That was a serious butt whipping I gave that nasty cracker."

"Yeah," Crystal Yelled from another cell down the hall. "It felt good kicking some behind."

"You alright Verna," Crystal yelled.

"Yeah, but it is dark down here."

"You will get used to it," Man said. "Don't be such a punk."

"But I am a punk," Verna said.

Man started laughing. "I saw you swinging. Who were you fighting a ghost?"

They all laughed.

"Hang in there," a familiar voice called from down the hall.

"Rose is that you," Verna yelled.

"The one and only," Rose called back.

"Well alright then," Man said. "What you doing down here, homey?"

"I knocked a CO on her butt the other day," Rose said. CO was the popular term used when referring to the guards. It was an abbreviation from their official title of Correctional Officer.

"Get out of here," Man said.

"Yeah I did," Rose said. "I will be down here for a minute but it sure will be worth it. I have wanted to get at that CO for a while. I heard about the rumble on your unit. I wish I could have been there. These white inmates think they are running something.

"What are we going to do down here," Verna asked?

"Nothing," Rose responded. "We just sit here in the hole and wait until our segregation time is up."

On the tenth day of being in the hole, Verna was brought out, showered and given clean state clothing.

"You are going before the parole board," the CO said.

At the parole board, Verna was asked a lot of questions. She was asked about the fight on her unit. She thought she would be denied first paper, as it was called when released your first time up for parole.

She was surprised at the words of the head of the parole board.

"You will probably be released even with the fight because you will serve your time for the fight in segregation. If we don't release you, you will mandatory out soon anyway and we need the space for more violent offenders. We can not release you to the streets. Do you have a resident where you can be released to? If not we will release you to a half way house." Verna had heard that half way houses were worst than prison. She would rather take her chances on the street. She gave them her Mother's and Stepdaddy's address in hopes that they would not check. The parole board told her they would review all the information and she would receive official notification within several weeks. She was returned to her cell in segregation.

"How did it go, sister," Rose asked?

"I think I am going to be released," Verna replied.

"Alright," Crystal said because I don't think you belong in here anyway."

Verna thought. I don't belong anywhere.

"Yeah," Man added. "We are not always going to be around to help your punk butt. Those girls will be looking for the opportunity to catch you by yourself."

Several days later, two male officers carried down a screaming white girl.

"Oh no," Man yelled. "Crazy Alice, why don't you take her crazy butt to the other side with the rest of the white girls?"

One of the officers said. "Now Man, don't start no mess. You know we don't discriminate. Those days are long gone."

"Yeah right," Verna said as she remembered the night she and Jay were arrested."

Crazy Alice was short, fat, and ugly. Her hair was broken off in various places. Her eyes revealed that she was insane. They literally threw Crazy Alice in the cell next to Verna. Crazy Alice started to scream for a cigarette.

"You don't get nothing," the officer told Crazy Alice.

Rose said. "Give the girl a cigarette so she can shut her mouth up."

A big female officer came down to the basement. She stepped up to Rose's cell. "You know the rules. No cigarettes for isolation and segregation inmates. So shut your mouth."

"Being state struck can put you in a bind," Rose said.

"Yeah, and being a convict put you in prison," she said to Rose.

"But I won't be in here forever," Rose said with anger.

"Is that a threat, convict?"

"Take it anyway you want to rent a cop."

"You just caught a charge." The officer smiled and walked away.

"Why you let that CO run you up on a charge," Man asked?

"Because uniform or not. I am not going to let nobody talk down to me like dirt."

Crystal joined in. "You played right into her hands. Now you will probably get another month down here in the hole."

"Yeah whatever," was Rose's reply.

"With an attitude like that you will probably be down here forever," Crystal said.

Before Rose could respond, Crazy Alice began yelling and banging on the cell bars for a cigarette.

"If I had a cigarette, I would give her my last cigarette so she would shut up," Man said. "Shut up, Alice!"

At lunch time, a new officer came down with lunch.

They heard Crazy Alice ask the new officer for a cigarette.

"No," the officer said.

"Then take this food," Alice yelled. She threw the food between the bars into the hallway.

"You get no more food," the officer said.

"I am sick," Alice said. "I am constipated and I demand medical treatment. I need a laxative."

"If you promise to be quiet, I will bring you a laxative," The officer said.

Alice calmed down. "I need two doses because one dose don't do nothing for me."

The officer was glad Alice had calmed down. "I will bring you two doses but you have to stay quiet."

Man protested. "Don't bring that crazy girl no laxatives."

"I can't deny her medication. Anyway mind your own business and let me do my job."

"I'm chillin; I was only trying to help."

143

"I don't remember asking for no convict's help," the officer said as she walked up the steps.

"See what I mean they treat us like dirt," Rose said.

"They may talk to me like dirt," Man responded. "But I ain't going to catch no bull charge. The way I see it I am just going to sit and wait and see if I run into any of them on the streets. Then I can see how nasty they can be."

The officer came down with two cups of milk of magnesia.

"Oh Lord," Man said. "Not two cups. You guys better breathe now while you can."

Verna was confused. "Why?"

"You will see," Rose said laughing.

Crazy Alice was quiet for about two hours. Verna could hear Crazy Alice straining every now and then. She thought the crazy girl was serious. She is constipated.

An hour later Verna began to smell the most awful smell.

Man yelled. "Everybody hold your nose."

Verna did not understand. "What's going on?"

Everyone started laughing at Verna's first experience with Crazy Alice.

To Verna the smell was unbearable. "I know it is supposed to stink but don't it supposed to go away after a while?"

Verna could hear Rose, Crystal, and Man laughing at her.

Verna became nauseated. She barely made it to the toilet beside her bed before she started vomiting.

"Baby, you got a weak stomach," Man yelled still laughing.

But after two hours of the smell, no one thought it was funny anymore.

Verna heard someone throwing up and gagging. "Who that," Verna asked?

"Not me," Rose said not laughing anymore.

"It's not me," Crystal said. "But it will be me soon because I can't stand this much longer."

"Man, I know that ain't you," Rose asked?

"Shut up," Man said gagging.

Rose jumped on the opportunity to have something on Man.

"Yeah stick girl you bleed every month just like the rest of us."

"If any one of you tell anybody about this, you can forget about me protecting you," Man said.

"Don't worry about Rose," Crystal said to Man. "Stink like this will make King Kong gag."

Rose started laughing. "Yeah Crystal you just down with Man because she protects you from that big old butch girl that keep running you down and," before Rose could finish her statement, a strong wave of nausea overcame her. She tried to stop it but it all came up at once. She did not even make it to the toilet.

For the moment, Crystal and Man forgot about the smell and started laughing at Rose. Even Verna found herself laughing.

"I know you not laughing, Verna," Rose said.

"You asked for that," Crystal said.

"What is really going on with the smell," Verna asked?

Crystal explained. "When Crazy Alice gets mad, she rubs her own feces all over the walls of her cell."

"How can she stand it," Verna asked?

"The girl is crazy," Man said.

"What are we going to do," Verna asked?

"The only thing we can do is wait until the officer makes rounds."

As Man was speaking, the same officer who had given Crazy

Alice the laxatives came down the steps to make rounds. "What the heck," the officer said in surprise.

"Because of you Crazy Alice gone and rubbed her bowels all on the walls," Rose said.

The officer started to walk back up the steps.

"Wait," Man yelled. "I have rights. I am not going to live in these conditions. Either somebody going to move me or get that crazy girl up out of here."

"I will see what I can do," the officer said gagging.

"I want a grievance," Rose demanded.

"Yeah I want to see the Warden," Crystal joined in.

The officer came back down with two male sergeants. Sgt. Roberts was a middle aged handsome Sergeant that all the girls were crazy about. "Whoa," he said holding his nose. "I see Crazy Alice is at it again."

The female officer walked near Crazy Alice's cell to pick up the tray she had earlier thrown on the floor. Crazy Alice ran to her bars and through a cup of piss on the female officer. "I told you I want a cigarette."

Man, Crystal, Rose and Verna all started laughing. The female officer was yelling. "She threw piss on me." Sgt. Roberts tried to calm her down. "Go on and check out and get yourself together. These things happen." The female officer ran up the stairs in tears.

"What you going to do about this," Crystal asked Sgt. Roberts.

"Chill baby," Sgt. Roberts said. "We are going to ship her butt out of here tomorrow to Northern State Mental Hospital."

"What about tonight," Man asked.

"We are going to hose down the area. She can't have much more in her. I don't care how much laxative she took. We will keep the area hosed down. We will get some air freshener down here. Meanwhile I will arrange to get you girls out on the segregation ball field for a couple of hours while we hose the area down and try to freshen it up some for you girls."

"That will work," Man said.

"Now you talking," Rose joined in.

"I am down with that," Verna said gagging. "But make it quick."

True to his word, Sgt. Roberts arranged for them to have recreation outside. They were given their meals outside. When they returned the area had been hosed down and air freshener had been sprayed. Each cell had a bottle of air freshener in it. There still lingered a faint smell in the air, but compared to how it had been this was much better. They each knew that some officers would have left them down there to deal with the smell and Crazy Alice. The next morning when they woke up, Crazy Alice and the smell was gone. The female Correctional Officer never returned to work.

Several weeks had passed. Verna was still in segregation. She had not heard from the parole board. She was worried. During the fifth week, she received legal mail. As Verna read the mail, she jumped and screamed out in joy. "I made it. I made first papers!" Everyone shouted with her.

"When your date," Rose asked.

"The 22nd," Verna said.

"That's tomorrow," Crystal said.

Verna felt a wave of nausea. She thought she would pass out from excitement. It was too much for one day. She did not think about she had nowhere to go. She only thought about getting out of there. Crystal cut through Verna's thoughts. "Make sure you write us girl."

"You know I will."

The next morning as Verna was being led out by an officer, she stopped by Crystal's cell first. "I will write you."

"I know you will," Crystal said.

Next, she stopped by Man's cell. "Thanks for looking out for me. You may be different, but you are worth more than a pot of gold to me and I will miss you."

"Don't come back baby," Man said.

"I won't," Verna said.

Last Verna stopped at Rose's cell. "Rose I never would have made it without you. You are so special to me. If you ever need anything and I have it then it is yours."

"Just hang in there sister," Rose said with tears in her eyes.

As Verna left the prison, she felt happiness that she was leaving. She was also sad because inside she had found true friendship. Something she had not had since Sue Kinley.

JOY

Joy felt led to move her headquarters from Atlanta to her hometown in Detroit. She wanted to be near Mama Mae who was getting too old to travel to Atlanta to see her. She also wanted to be more active in the search for Verna. She had one of the best Private Investigators on the case, but thought that being on the streets so much would increase her chances of finding her sister. Joy had finished speaking at two speaking engagements at State University in Detroit. She was tired. She and her staff had been working the streets 12-14 hours a day. Her popularity had grown and newspapers and magazines were frequently asking her for interviews. After her speech, she was happy to return to her luxury suite. She had come a long way. She now rode in limousines. Her suite included a large lounging area, master bedroom, luxury bathroom, which included a full spa. She was blessed. Joy turned on the central music system. Quickly the sounds of soft jazz filled the entire suite. She was about to drift off to sleep when the front desk called her. "Ms. Edwards, we have a young man down here who says he is your brother."

"I have not seen my brother in years. Ask him his name."

"He says Junior."

Joy was excited. "Send him up."

Joy waited at the door. For some reason she expected to see a young boy come to the door.

Instead she saw a tall, handsome young man of about nineteen.

"Junior," she asked unsure.

Junior walked up to Joy and hugged her. They held on to each other for a long time.

"Come in," Joy said.

"Joy," he said.

Joy was surprised at the deepness of his voice. "I heard you speak at the University. I am proud to tell everyone you are my sister. I

have been following your program and progress from the very
beginning."

Joy was surprised. "Why didn't you call me?"

"I was afraid."

"Afraid of what? You are my brother."

"I let you down."

"No," Joy said.

"I did not protect you from my father."

"You were only a child. There was nothing you could do."

"I hate that man's blood runs through me," Junior said.

Joy changed the subject. "How are Mama and Precious?"

"Mama spends all her time doing all she can for my Father and
Precious. Precious is still smart as ever. She has already been
awarded two scholarships. She is a whiz in the music
department."

"That's great," Joy said.

Joy became serious. She had to ask the question. Her heart began
to pound. "Stepdaddy doesn't touch her does he?"

"No, he knows Mama would kill him and if she did not kill him I would. That man will never touch another one of my sisters again. The only thing he touches now is a bottle."

"Tell me about yourself," Joy encouraged.

"This is my second year at State University on a basketball scholarship. Come see me play sometime."

"Of course I will. Do you need anything?"

"No, I am doing fine. I have a part time job."

"Let me give you some money."

"I don't need any money. I have to go to practice now. Can I come see you or call sometime?"

"You had better," Joy said.

Joy wrote down her home number. She also wrote down her office phone number and address. "I am on the streets most of the time, but you can leave a message with my answering service. I will definitely get back with you."

"Promise," he asked.

"With all my heart." She smiled giving him a hug. "You sure are handsome. I bet you have a lot of girlfriends."

"Just one. She majors in counseling. You are her idol. She will be very angry with me if I don't introduce you to her."

Joy smiled. "I tell you what, when is your next game?"

"Next Friday."

"I will be there. Afterwards, I would like to take both of you to dinner."

"Deal," Junior said.

As Junior walked to the elevator, he stopped.

"What's wrong," Joy asked?

"Why haven't you asked," he said?

"Asked What?"

"About her," Junior said.

"Because I am afraid to ask. I am afraid of what you might tell me."

"She came back for you," Junior said.

"She's alive," Joy asked.

"It was several years ago, but she came back for you Joy."

"Do you know where she is," Joy asked? Her heart was beating so fast in anticipation of his answer.

"No, I don't know where she is. Like a young fool, I ran away from her in shame."

"Why were you in shame, Junior?"

"Shame for not being a man."

"But you were only a little boy."

"Still I should have helped you, Joy."

"You have to let that go," Joy said. "You are a young man. You have your own life to live now. He may be your Father but you are a different man than he is."

Junior smiled, "I am glad I finally had the courage to come see you."

"Me too," Joy said.

Joy watched Junior walk away. Seeing him made her sad. She thought about all the unhappy times she had at home. She thought about how she and Verna had been an outcast. She thought how Verna had told her she was her Joy in the morning. She went to her suitcase and pulled out the picture of Verna that she always took with her no matter where she traveled. She remembered smashing it so many years ago. It was now in a very nice frame.

She thought. Where are you, Verna. Why can't we find each

other?

VERNA

Verna registered herself at the same Salvation Army where she had met Jay and Dee. There was a different lady at the front desk. She was very nice to Verna. The center looked much better it had been renovated. They no longer placed people in the open area where Verna had spent the night during her previous stay. Now that area was an actual gym. This time Verna was placed in a small room with two single beds in it. She did not have a room mate. Verna was told that the Center was not as crowded as it used to be because of the many new programs and shelters now available for the homeless. Apparently the city had come under fire by grass root groups who brought attention to the city's large homeless population and the lack of shelters and programs. Verna had kicked her drug habit the hard way while incarcerated. There were all types of drugs available in prison for the right cash or the right amount of cigarettes. Since Verna had no family to send her money for her prison account, she was unable to purchase cigarettes from the canteen. Cash was prohibited in prison. However, many of the women found ways to get cash on the inside. Verna had earned $400.00 from working at the laundry in prison. Prison pay was very low. She only made twenty eight cents an hour. Money earned by prisoners was held in a special account until the inmates were released. Verna used $200.00 of the money to buy some clothes, as she had no clothing, only what she was incarcerated in. Verna felt that she would look for a job. She earned her High School Diploma while incarcerated. Although she was incarcerated less than a year, she was enrolled in a program where she was allowed to work at her own pace. Since Verna had made it to the 10th grade in school she was far more advanced than most of the women. Many of them never graduated from Middle school. Verna was very proud of her diploma. She thought about asking O'Neill for her job back. She knew in her heart she should apologize and explain to O'Neill her problems. She walked to O'Neill's and was surprised to see the building boarded up and closed down. As she walked back to the Center she ran into one of Jay's old drug contacts. He gave Verna a small piece of crack cocaine as a welcome back home gift. She did not want to take it, but he insisted and told her she did not want to insult his generosity. He told her if she ever wanted to sell a little something he could hook her up and she knew where to find him. The crack remained in a little piece of plastic wrap in her night stand drawer for days. For two days she put in applications at different stores and restaurants. She soon found that the diploma she was so proud of was nothing but a piece of paper for her. She could not get around the question about being convicted of a crime. She could not lie because all the applications included her signature for a background check. She became very frustrated. Two weeks later there was still no job offers. She received a letter from the Department of Corrections denying her request to visit Jay in prison. The letter stated that since she was a recent released ex felon that she would have to wait a year to even submit a request to be considered to visit Jay and even then, it would be at the discretion of the Department of Corrections. She was devastated. She remembered the crack and how it made her forget her problems. Right now she needed to forget. She thought just this one time. She took the crack out of the drawer. She did not have a pipe so she used an old coke can. She felt so good. She felt as if an old friend whom she had not seen in a long time had come to visit her. She did not think about any of her problems only about how good she felt. Verna quickly found Jay's old contact, Too Short. She gave him her remaining $200.00 she was saving until she got a job. He asked her what she was going to do with all that dope. She told him she could not get a job because of her record and needed to sell it to earn money. She told herself she would smoke this and then that would be it. In two days she was back asking Too Short for more dope. As Verna approached, Too Short smiled. "I was expecting you baby, but not so soon. What you need?"

"I need about a fifty piece."

Too Short continued to smile. "Where your money? You know I can't be giving you my stuff for free."

Too Short admired her tall slim body. "What can you give me?"

"I can work for you," Verna said.

"What do you know about selling? Jay handled most of that. You were just his pretty little trophy."

Verna dropped her head. "I need it, Too Short."

Too Short was not really short. Verna did not know how he got his street name. He was at least six feet tall. He had a bald head and dark skin. He would not be considered attractive until he smiled. When he smiled he had even white teeth with one gold tooth. When he smiled his big eyes lit up. His smile was deceiving. He was a very conniving person. He continued to flash his smile at Verna. "I tell you what, you still living down at the Salvation Army?"

"Yes," Verna said.

"You can set business up for me in there. I hear crack heads crashing out in there all the time. I'm a nice guy and Jay was my boy so I will give you twenty percent of what you sell plus your own supply for personal use because I don't want you smoking up my stuff."

Verna felt she had no choice. Plus she could earn a little money.

Too Short handed her a small package of crack. "This is just a little bit. I want to see how you do before I go giving you a whole lot of my dope."

"What about me," Verna asked.

Too Short handed her another small pocket. Verna started to walk away. She needed to get somewhere so she could smoke. Too Short grabbed her arm. She winced in pain at the tightness of his grip. "Listen, I don't usually trust my stuff to no users. Don't mess over my stuff. The only reason I am dealing with you is because Jay is my homeboy. Remember if you mess over me, I will not hesitate to cut you down, homeboy or not."

He released his grip and began to stroke where his hand had been. "Who knows I don't usually keep no crack using female as my woman but I just might try you."

Verna hurried away. She went to the nearest gas station. She locked herself in the outside bathroom. She now had a pipe. By the time of her second hit she had already forgotten what Too Short had said.

JOY

It felt good being home. Joy sat eating an early dinner with Ma
Mae, Sam, Junior, and his girlfriend Renee. State University was
out for summer break. Junior and Renee' were now traveling with
Joy on her speaking engagements. They were home for a few days
between engagements. Joy would be appearing on a local talk
show. This was part of a promotion for a highly published
speaking engagement that would take place at the city square
three days from today.

Renee said, "I have not tasted food like this since growing up in
Mississippi."

They ate pork barbequed spare ribs, collard greens seasoned with ham hocks, potatoe salad, and chitterlings.

"The food is good," Sam said with a mouth full of food. "But I don't eat nobody's chitterlings."

"Don't try to be cute," Mae said. "You know you always asking me when I'm going to cook some chitterlings."

Sam laughed. "You busted me. Pass me some more of them hog guts."

Ma Mae laughed. She spoke to Joy. "I m sure glad to meet your brother and his girlfriend, she right pretty."

Renee smiled. "Thank you Ms. Mae."

Mae addressed Junior. "Boy, you better hold on to this girl. She seem like she make you a good woman."

Junior smiled. "Yeah I am looking forward to that."

Renee nudged Junior.

"I guess we better get ready to go to the studio," Joy said.

"Lord have mercy," Mae said. "I ain't never been to no talk show. Chile what am I gonna wear?"

Renee responded. "Don't worry Ms. Mae. We will help you get ready."

The women got up to clean the dishes.

"No," Junior said. "We know how long it takes women to get dressed. Me and Sam will do the dishes. You fine girls go ahead and get dressed."

When the women had left, Sam looked at Junior, irritated. "Now why did you go and do that? I don't wash no dishes."

Junior laughed. "Little suds won't melt you, old man."

"Yeah," Sam said. "But I will clean the pot of chitterlings." He winked.

JOY AND VERNA

Verna was sitting in the recreation area of the Salvation Army watching television. For the past several months she had been selling crack regularly. Too Short was right business at the Center was good. Once the word was out the addicts came to her. Too Short had not noticed yet, but she had been using hers and pinching a little bit of his too. She was just about to go to her room and smoke some crack, when she heard a local talk show host announce the day's guest.

"Joy Edwards," the talk show host announced.

For the first time since she relapsed, the thought of crack left Verna's mind. She looked up at the screen to see a beautiful brown skinned woman who undeniably was her sister.

"Joy," Verna yelled out in excitement. There were a few residents in the recreation room who turned to look at Verna as if she was insane.

"That's my sister," Verna yelled.

"Yeah right," someone said. "She is a well known advocate against drug use. Looks like you could stand to watch this show."

Verna cried throughout the entire show. She listened to Joy talk about her outreach program and how effective it is.

Verna thought. Joy you made it. Here you are a well respected person and I, your sister, stand for all you work so hard against.

Verna learned that Joy would be speaking the next day at City Square, which was only two blocks away.

Verna ran to her room and counted the money she had made selling crack that day. She had two hundred dollars. She knew it was Too Short's money, but she did not care. She went to the mall and bought a new outfit. She did not know she had lost so much weight. It took her two hours and seventy-five dollars to find a beige skirt suit that looked decent on her skinny frame. She

thought back when her body was considered appealing. Her once

shapely legs were now skin and bones. She spent fifty dollars on a

matching pair of shoes. She went to the beauty salon and had her

nappy matted hair cut, pressed, and curled.

"It's not much I can do with it sister. You have let it go so bad.

But it still looks decent. You are on that stuff I can see that," the

beautician said.

Verna paid the beautician fifty dollars.

"Thanks," Verna said as she walked out.

"Get yourself together sister," the beautician yelled after Verna.

The next morning Verna got up early so that she could be the first

one in the shower. She could not believe how dirty she was. She

could not remember the last time she had taken a shower. She

dressed in her new outfit and matching shoes. "I don't look so

bad," she said to herself.

She picked up her crack pipe and was about to light it when she

thought about Joy and all that she stood for. "Get yourself

together." The beautician had said.

Verna threw the pipe in the trash can. "This is what you stand for, Joy," she said aloud.

When Verna arrived at City Square, it was already packed. She squeezed in as close as she could get to the platform which was about one hundred feet away. Verna knew that Joy was approaching by the sound of the loud applause. She was very excited. I finally found you, she thought.

When Joy took the microphone, Verna could not believe how beautiful she had become.

"Good Morning friends," Joy said. Joy's voice had not changed. The sound of Joy's voice made Verna remember all the special talks they shared as children.

"It's good to be home," Verna heard Joy say. "First of all, I want to introduce you to my mother Mae and my father Sam. Verna was confused. Who were these people Joy referred to as her mother and father? She could sense that there was a lot of love between them. "I would also like to introduce my brother Junior and his fiancée, Renee. Verna could not believe this handsome young man was the little boy who had ran away from her years

172

ago. She found herself wiping her eyes. They had turned out alright. She was a nobody. She was planning on fighting her way up to Joy after the speech even if it took all day. How could she, a crack addict, face these fine people? They were her family yet she had no place with them. She would not embarrass them.

"I am not going to speak long," Joy said. "I am here to give every crack user in the city an invitation. I want you to know that I am not ashamed of you. I want everyone to spread the word. Tomorrow night at 9:00 p.m. at the Gallery Hotel Ballroom. I want all crack users to attend. It does not matter if you are only using a little bit. I want you to bring your friends who are too strung out to make it on their own. Mothers bring your sons and daughters. Sisters bring your brothers. Brothers bring your sisters. There will be no crack offered. There will be plenty of good food and lots of love. My people have been out on these streets the past few days spreading the word. I am not asking anything from any of you, just come. If you feel uncomfortable then you can leave. I and my people will be there among you. You can come talk to us. We will let you know how to find help. This is the first time I have tried this. I know it can work. Please come I am begging you." The crowd gasped as Joy dropped to her knees. They were moved at the amount of compassion she had for them. "I am not too proud to beg. If it saves one life, I will beg. You my friends, are worth it. Let me help you find your worth. You are precious to me and to God." Joy stood up. "I want to ask all of you out there to come forward if you need help today. Come to me now. Form a line to the side. You don't have to wait until tomorrow. For some of you tomorrow will be too late."

Verna was astonished as she watched the mass of people slowly move to the side. Many had tears in their eyes. Joy continued. "My friends help the ones who are too weak to make it on their own. If you need help raise your hand and someone will help you.

Verna heard someone next to her yell out, "Here's one sister Joy!" Verna felt someone shove her forward.

Joy and Verna's eyes locked for a brief moment. Joy's eyes continued to roam the crowd. Verna's eyes clouded with tears. Joy did not even know her. Joy did not know what it was, but she felt something the instant she had looked at the worn out addict in the crowd. She turned her attention back to the addict to see the back of the addict as she was leaving. Verna turned around to get one last look at her beloved sister. She knew in her heart that Joy would always be her sister, her Joy in the morning. She also knew that they could never be together again. Verna looked up into large slanted eyes that were a mirror of her own eyes. She saw Joy's head shake from side to side as in disbelief. Verna turned and quickly worked her way through the crowd away from the platform and Joy.

"Wait," Joy yelled into the microphone. "I have been looking for you. Someone stop that woman in the beige skirt suit." Verna felt hands grasping at her, but she was able to work her way out of the crowd. Junior was quickly trying to work his way through the crowd to catch Verna.

Verna continued to run without stopping. She did not know where she got the strength and energy from. She could hear Junior yelling. "Verna stop, it's me Junior!"

She ducked into an old abandoned house. As she peeped out, she could see Junior. He stopped in front of the old abandoned house. He was yelling her name in a panic. Verna wanted to call out to him. She was frozen in shock and shame. She slipped through the back door. As she ran through the back door, she could hear Junior calling her name in desperation.

Verna made it to the Salvation Army. She felt as if she had been beat with a fifty pound brick. She sank down on her bed. She went to the trash can and grabbed the pipe and crack. Her hands were trembling. As she smoked the crack, she expected her troubles to go away but no matter how much she smoked, she still felt an ache right in the middle of her heart.

Joy was running around in a panic. She and Junior had been out looking for Verna. She was having a meeting with three top detectives in the area. "I know she is here," Joy said. "I want you to find my sister. No matter how much it cost, find my sister."

Joy's dinner had gone well! Two hundred had shown up. Out of two hundred, ninety five had asked for help. The Governor had commended her and invited her to dinner. She was surprised at how handsome the Governor was in person. He was twice her age but she found herself attracted to him. He was tall and had the build of a football player. He was golden tan in complexion. He had small intelligent eyes that were hidden by glasses. His hair was black and wavy with a touch of grey. "You seem happy with your work," he said.

"I am very happy with my work."

"But are you happy?"

Joy told him about Verna.

"I would love to help you find your sister on one condition."

"What condition," Joy asked alarmed.

"If you will have dinner with me again next week."

"I would love to." Joy smiled.

The Governor was true to his word. He put out an APB on Verna. He also offered a reward of five thousand dollars to anyone providing information leading to the whereabouts of Verna. Joy made a vow that she would not leave the area until she found Verna. She cancelled all speaking engagements.

Three weeks passed when Joy received a call from one of her detectives saying that Verna was staying at the local Salvation Army Homeless Center. She and Junior quickly headed to the center. When Joy and Junior arrived at the center, they were told that Verna was staying there but was not in the center at the

moment. Joy called the Governor and told him her news. He met

Joy and Junior at the center. They were allowed to wait in Verna's

room. Joy saw the pipe that Verna used on her bed. She picked it

up and rubbed where Verna's mouth had been so many times.

Somehow the press found out what was going on. Three camera

crews from the local news networks arrived. Joy was afraid they

would frighten Verna away. She did not want to lose her again.

"Get them out of here. They may frighten her away," she ordered.

"Mam, this is a news breaking story," one of them said.

The Governor cut him off. "Look man, all of you leave right now.

If you frighten her, there will be no story. We will call a press

conference later."

The news crew was persistent. "Can we leave our writers here if

they promise to stay out of the way?"

The Governor agreed. He put his arm around Joy. "She won't get

away this time."

Joy felt flushed. It was obvious that Verna had changed. What if

she did not want to be with her? She pushed the thought out of

her mind. The Director of the Salvation Army was called in when he found out the Governor was at his center. They waited for three

hours. It was 10:00p.m. Verna had not arrived. "She will be here,"

the Director said. "As I understand she has nowhere else to go."

Joy felt the need to be alone. "If you don't mind I would like to sit

here in her room by myself. Please everyone wait outside."

Junior hugged Joy. "We will all wait in the recreation room. I

think that would be best. We don't want to spook her."

Joy sat alone in Verna's room. So many years had passed. She

slowly walked around the small room. She touched places where

Verna may have touched. "I finally found you."

Verna sat in the living room of a very well furnished apartment.

Too Short was standing over her. "Where is my money," he

demanded.

"I don't know," Verna whimpered.

"What did I tell you? Where is my dope? You used it didn't you?

You did not sell any of it?" Too Short was yelling in her face,

furiously.

Verna was quiet. Too Short slapped her face. His gold ring cut her face. Instinctively, she reached up to feel the warm blood drip down her face.

"I'll get your money, Too Short."

"Crack head," he yelled over and over again. He began to hit her with his fist. Verna felt her face begin to swell. She opened her mouth to scream.

"If you scream I will kill you crack head. I am going to get paid one way or another." He reached down and unzipped his pants. Verna cringed in fear. "O.k., but please don't hurt me." Verna slipped out of her dirty dress. Too Short shook his head in disgust. "You're pathetic. I remember when you were fine. You're so disgusting I can't even mess with you. Get out of my face. Get out there and turn some tricks or something and get me my money. If you don't get me my money I will kill you."

Verna stumbled out the door. She slowly made her way back to the Center. When she got to the door, she almost turned around but something inside seemed to draw her inside. As Verna walked by the recreation room, she quickly glimpsed a few unfamiliar faces. This did not alarm her. She was used to strange people sent by the State to observe at the Center. The strangers were too engrossed in their own thoughts and conversation to even notice her. Verna was too busy trying to get by unnoticed that she did not recognize Junior in the group.

Good, she thought. She did not want to be bothered with questions about how good the Center treated her. Her face was a bloody mess. She needed to get to her room and see how bad her face was. She put her hand on the door knob. She jerked her hand back. She could sense someone inside. She thought. I guess they finally gave me a roommate. That's all I need. She walked in to face the back of a well dressed woman. She could see her pipe in the woman's hand.

"Hey, put that down," Verna yelled!

Joy turned around. She was crying. "Please don't run."

Verna turned her face away in shame. Joy went to her and turned her beaten face toward hers. Verna threw her arms around Joy. She was sobbing uncontrollably. Joy pulled back. She held up the pipe. She walked and threw the pipe in the trash can. "You don't need this anymore. You have me. Your Joy is back."

Junior walked into the room. He paused. He ran and grabbed Verna. He began to cry as all three held on to each other.

Verna was taken to the hospital for observation for a few days. Joy remained by her side the entire time. Every time Verna felt the familiar urge to do crack, she would grab Joy's hand to make sure Joy was still there. Verna's plight made the news headlines. Every station was talking about how Joy Edwards had found her long lost sister beaten and strung out on drugs. The Governor sent Verna some flowers. People who worked with Joy came to see Verna. They counseled her and encouraged her to be strong. During Verna's second day at the hospital, Junior came in with two beautiful girls. He introduced the brown skinned one as his fiancée. The second girl was a young teenager. She was beautiful with long silky jet black hair. She was fair skin and had grey eyes. Verna whispered to Joy. "Who is she?"

"I don't know," Joy replied.

The young girl seemed quite shy. She went to Verna and gave her a dozen roses. Verna was touched. This stranger seemed to really care about her. The young girl went to Joy and gave her a hug.

Joy was startled. Something about her seemed very familiar.

Junior laughed. "Don't you two know your own baby sister?"

"I can't believe we have such a beautiful sister," Joy said happily.

Precious walked back and stood closely beside Junior. "I guess

you can see she is shy," Junior said. "She will be fine once she get

to know you."

Joy was saddened by the thought that her own sister would have

to get to know her. They had never been close. Precious was her

Mama's baby and she was always up under their Mother.

"Precious has to go to music lessons," Junior said. "I promised

Mom I would take her."

The mention of their Mother really disturbed Joy. She could not

help but be resentful. She wondered how their Mother could allow

the things that happened to her and Verna to happen. She blamed

her Mother for Verna's addiction.

"I will take Precious. You stay with your sisters," Renee said to

Junior.

"Thanks," Junior said. Renee led Precious out of the hospital

room.

Verna could not contain herself. Just as Joy had to know, she had to be sure. "Stepdaddy never touched her, did he? She is so pretty."

"No, he never did," Junior said.

"Are you sure?" Verna asked in pain.

"Yes, I am sure. Let's not talk about Precious. You will have time to get to know her."

Joy interrupted, "Does Mama and Stepdaddy know Precious was here?"

"No they do not but Precious wanted to see you and Verna."

Verna dropped her head. It really bothered her that her own Mother cared so little about her. Joy could sense the pain in Verna. She once felt the same pain. She no longer felt the pain only a nagging ache at times. She now felt that Mama Mae and Sam were her parents. She wished she could share their love with Verna so that she could feel the love of real parents.

Junior interrupted their thoughts. "Verna, tell us what happened to you all these years. Tell us who did this to you."

Verna thought back to being homeless and penniless. She thought about Jay and Dee. She thought about life in prison and finally she thought about Too Short and his promise to hurt her if she did not get his money. "I don't want to talk about it now. I just want to forget about that life."

"I need to know why you ran away from us, Junior insisted."

Joy interrupted Junior. "Why don't we give her time to recuperate and heal? There will be time for questions later."

Junior was irritated. "Only if she promises never to run away again."

Verna promised.

Junior excused himself to go play basketball. Verna and Joy were left alone. Verna started crying. She did not make a sound but the tears would not stop. Joy laid down in the bed with her and held her. "Just get it all out," Joy said.

"I'm so sorry," Verna cried. "I did not know. Stepdaddy promised. I would have never left you if I knew he would do that to you."

"Shh," Joy said. "It is not your fault. I have healed. Now it is your time to heal."

After three days, Joy took Verna home to Mama Mae. Joy had told Verna all about her adopted Mother. She told her how Mama Mae had told her that she would see her again. She told her how Mama Mae had prayed with her whenever she would feel discouraged. She told her how Mama Mae taught her about the love of God and how God's love had changed her life and gave her the strength and faith she needed to continue on.

When Verna walked in the home, Mama Mae grabbed and hugged her. "I can see you are my Joy's sister. Honey, you is skinny but I will take care of that in no time." As the weeks passed, with the help of Joy's love and Mama Mae's cooking, Verna began to look and feel better. State University began the fall session and Junior and his fiancé returned to school. Verna began to travel with Joy a great deal. She loved the feeling she felt when Joy introduced her. Everyone would stand and applause. Joy purchased a huge five bedroom house for her and Joy. She did this in hopes one day Mama Mae and Sam would come and live with her but they were stubborn and refused. They would often come over and cook for Verna and Joy. Every now and then Junior would bring Precious to the house to visit. However, Precious continued to be quiet and shy staying up under Junior. After eight months in recovery, Verna asked Joy could she work the streets with Joy and her assistants. Joy was hesitant. "I don't think it is a good idea for you to return to the streets."

Verna insisted. "It is time I do my share. I am strong enough. This is what I want to do."

Verna started out working with Joy and two other group members. They normally tried to counsel in groups of four on the streets. Verna was amazed at how easy it was to use her personal experiences to help others. She knew what they were going through. Many of them who knew her from the streets were amazed at the change in Verna. This left a positive impact on the addicts. They remembered Verna at her worst. Verna knew that contrary to popular beliefs no addict wanted to be an addict. Verna was able to take Joy's group to areas in the community where most of the addicts hung out. They were bringing in dozens of addicts each day.

Joy, Verna, John, and Junior were working the streets early one evening. Junior was home on school break. Often he would go out with Joy's group. John was a recovering crack addict. Although he had been clean for six years he knew that there was no such thing as a recovered addict. John had been working with Joy since the program began in Atlanta. The group approached a corner where a young woman in her late teens was standing. She was an obvious prostitute.

"Hey Sister," Joy said as they approached.

The young woman made it obvious that she did not want to be bothered. "Look, I know who you people are. Leave me alone. I don't want no help."

John took the lead. "Sister, I once felt that way myself."

"You don't know me. Leave me alone," she yelled.

Verna stepped up. "Sister, I stood on these same streets. I know that you are crying out for someone to help you. Isn't that right?"

The young woman looked at Verna. Everyone in the group was trained to back down if it seemed as if one person was getting through.

Verna continued, "I have felt the pain, Sister. I know you want to let it go but you are afraid. There is nothing worst than the fear of letting go because if you let it go, you will be faced with reality

and right now reality don't look so good to you, right?"

The young woman shook her head no.

Verna could see tears in the young woman's eyes. Verna reached

out for her hand but the young woman snatched her hand away

from Verna.

"Give me your hand," Verna said. "I was afraid of reality but hey

reality is not so bad once you deal with the pain. I know the voice

of pain is very loud, but after a while the voice gets softer and

softer and soon you don't hear it anymore. Every now and then

you hear a tiny whisper, but you know we have the power over

that whisper, so that it can never become a powerful voice ever

again, just a soft harmless whisper." Verna lowered her voice to a

whisper. "A soft harmless whisper."

Verna reached for the young woman's hand again. This time the

young woman did not snatch her hand away.

"What's your name," Verna asked the young woman?

"Betty."

The group was startled to hear a male voice yell from behind

them. "Betty, these people bothering you!"

Betty quickly snatched her hand away and wiped the tears from her eyes.

Verna was startled to see Too Short approach with his main partner Scorpion. Too Short did not recognize Verna.

"You got your money, Baby," Too Short asked Betty.

Betty handed Too Short some crumpled bills. He handed her a small rock.

Junior spoke up. "Look man, this sister wants help. Leave her alone, brother."

Too Short snapped. Who was this pretty boy? "First of all, I ain't your brother pretty boy."

Scorpion laughed. "These people got a nerve on our streets."

"These are not your streets," John said. "These streets belong to the people and community. We are going to take crack off our streets." Verna could tell that Too Short was getting very agitated.

"You had better leave before you find yourself deep in some stuff you don't want to be in and my stuff stinks."

Joy stepped up. "We are not leaving this young lady. She wants our help."

"Is that right," Too Short asked Betty.

"Naw, Too Short. I was just minding my business." Betty started walking away.

Verna knew that they should also be walking away. She knew how dangerous Too Short was. Scorpion was his trigger man and would turn violent at one word from Too Short. She wanted to encourage the group to move on but did not want to bring any attention to herself. Too Short still did not recognize her.

"Wait," Joy yelled after Betty. Too Short was tired of these people. He looked at Scorpion. "Yo Man, handle this."

Verna knew she had to get them out of there immediately. "We are out of here. We don't want any trouble."

For the first time Too Short took a close look at the quiet one. "Verna!" I don't believe it. I see you are fine again. I almost didn't recognize you and it would have been better for you if I had not. Yo Scorpion smoke this ho."

Everything seemed to go in slow motion but yet so fast. The group watched as Scorpion pulled out a semi automatic weapon and aimed point blank at Verna. Joy quickly jumped in front of

Verna. "No, she screamed!" Joy took two bullets in the chest. Verna was in shock. This had to be a dream. God let it be a dream. Instantly John and Junior both grabbed Scorpion and began to struggle with the gun. All three hit the pavement. Junior landed on top of Scorpion as the gun went flying. Quickly John ran to retrieve the gun. Verna was screaming. No one saw Too Short pull out a snub nose .38 Revolver. "Get off my boy," he yelled as he pointed the gun at Junior. He shot Junior in the head. Junior fell over on Scorpion. "Come on Scorpion," Too Short yelled as the sound of sirens was heard in the near distant. Scorpion rolled Junior off of him. John began firing wildly as Scorpion and Too Short began running. He had never shot a gun before and was surprised to see Scorpion fall to the pavement. He did not know it but he was crying. He knew that Joy and Junior had been hit. He continued to fire at Too Short. Too Short turned and fired hitting John in the arm. In spite of the pain, John continued to fire. Too Short hit the pavement, but stood back up and continued to run. John ran to Junior. Junior was not responding. Verna was hysterical. Verna was holding Joy. Blood was everywhere. Joy was barely conscious. Verna looked at John to find out about her brother. John shook his head. Verna saw him began to pray over Junior. She felt her only brother was gone. Verna continued to hold Joy.

"I'm dying," Joy said.

"No," yelled Verna becoming more hysterical.

Joy gained enough strength to speak. "Shut up," she said to Verna.

Verna was stunned.

"Junior is gone isn't he," Joy asked Verna?

Verna did not answer.

"Don't leave me," Verna cried.

"Listen my Sister," Joy said as she held on to life. She knew she was slipping away but she could not go until she said what she needed to say to Verna. "Promise you will listen."

"I will listen," Verna said through tears.

"Remember how you told me I am your joy in the morning?"

"I remember," Verna said.

Joy weakly continued. "You left me physically but we were always together. Do you agree with that?"

"Yes, I agree," Verna said crying.

Joy continued. "Now it is my time to leave you."

"No," Verna began.

Joy cut her off. "Be strong for me. Make me proud. Although I am leaving I will always be with you. I will always be your joy in the morning. Not even death can change that." Joy began to shake. "Hold me."

Verna held on tight. Verna grabbed her sister's hand. She felt Joy's hand loosening. "I see the light, Verna, it is beautiful. I am going to Jesus now. Joy was smiling. Then she slipped away. Verna continued to hold on to Joy. The paramedics came but Verna would not let go. John and a white police officer managed to gently pull Verna away. The paramedic felt for a pulse. There was no pulse. "There's no hurry on this one," he said. Ordinarily the police officer would not have cared about these people, but he knew who the deceased was. He had respect for her work. It's a shame he thought the very people she sought to help had led to her murder. "We are going to get everyone involved," he said with genuine conviction. "Do you know who did this? We got one of them. He is dead but there appears to have been another person involved by the trail of blood we see leaving the scene."

John looked at Verna. "Who is this Too Short?"

Verna was weak and in shock. She had lost her sister and brother in seconds and it was all her fault. She gave the officer Too Short's address.

"We are on this," he said to Verna. "I'm sorry."

A second ambulance had taken Junior away. Verna slowly began to walk away. "Wait," John yelled. "I can't let you leave alone like this." He started to follow Verna but a paramedic stopped him. "You have been shot." He led John into a waiting ambulance. John watched as Verna walked away.

Verna did not know how long she walked. She found herself at the corner of 5th Avenue and Lexington. This was an area where most addicts came to purchase crack. The word was out that Scorpion was dead and Too Short had been found bleeding in his apartment from a gunshot wound to the shoulder. He was expected to survive. He was taken to the hospital in police custody.

"Hey Lady," a young boy's voice said. "Are you lookin?"

"Yeah, I'm lookin," Verna said weakly. She handed the voice a fifty dollar bill. She walked to a near by park. She found an old can. She could hear the sound of the gun shots again and again in her head.

"Stop it," she yelled.

She quickly placed the crack on the can and prepared to smoke it.

"I have to make it stop," she said aloud.

It was getting dark. There were still a few people in the park. Verna did not care. The only thing she cared about now was making the pain go away. She searched her pockets for a lighter. She became frantic. Suddenly a young female voice asked? "You need a light lady?" Verna looked up to see a young girl of about seventeen standing over her. It was easy to see that the young girl was hurting for some dope.

"Here," the young girl said handing Verna a lighter. As Verna prepared to smoke the crack, the young girl asked, "You got a hit for me?" Verna heard Joy's voice. Be strong for me. She remembered all that Joy stood for. She took the can and threw it away from her.

"Why did you do that," the young girl asked? The young girl ran to where the can landed. She fell to her knees looking for the crack. Verna stood over the girl. "How long you been using, Sister?"

"Help me find it," the young girl pleaded. The young girl was desperate. "You got some more stuff, Lady?"

"I got some stuff better than crack," Verna said.

The young girl walked with Verna to a small diner near the park. Verna ordered food for them.

"Where the stuff at," the girl asked?

"First, what's your name," Verna asked?

"Mia," she said.

"My name is Verna and I want to help you get off of dope."

"What! You said you had some stuff!" The girl stood up and threw the food on the floor. "This is how much I feel about your help," she said spitting on the table. The young girl ran out the diner.

Verna had lost this one but she knew that there were many more people out on the streets who needed help. She knew she would continue Joy's work. She would do it for her Joy in the morning.

197

As Verna stood up to leave, a tall man in the diner approached her. He seemed almost seven feet tall. He was the most beautiful man she had ever seen. His eyes were the strangest blue. They appeared to look through her. "I saw how you tried to help that lost young lady," he said.

"I did not help her."

"Oh, but you did."

"How do you know," Verna asked?

"I know," he said.

"How can I help you," he continued?

"The only one who can help me now is God."

"Only God can help you," he said.

"Go to the hospital," he continued. Then he walked away.

Verna did not understand why she just knew that she had to do what this beautiful man had told her.

Joy's lifeless body was lifted into the ambulance. The paramedic riding in the rear thought what a tragic lost as he looked at this beautiful corpse. He thought he heard a breath. No, it couldn't be.

He thought he saw movement of her bloody chest. He leaned closer. He jumped as Joy gasped for air. He banged on the window. "Get a move on. She's alive," he yelled to the driver as he began to work on her. As the ambulance carrying Joy arrived at the hospital, the ambulance with Junior was speeding in. They quickly rolled Junior out. A team of doctors were standing by waiting for Junior. They had a team of trauma surgeons waiting in an operating room. John had also been brought in. He was stretched out on a hospital bed waiting to be prepped for surgery to remove the bullet out of his arm. He was in the operating room next to where they wheeled Junior. He saw the paramedics rush Junior by him. He jumped up from his bed in excitement. "He's alive!" A nurse quickly calmed John down. She addressed John. "We will have to move you to another surgery room. The surgeons need this room. They are bringing a young lady in with gunshot wounds to the chest. She is a famous advocate for drug addicts. She is barely hanging on. It is a miracle." John jumped up again. "What's her name," he yelled!

The nurse tried to get John to lie back down. He was jumping up. "Who is she?"

They rolled Joy in as they were working on her. John was screaming, "Thank you God!"

The doctors yelled, "Get him out of here." The nurse had to lead John out. He would not stay still. He asked the nurse what happened. He told the nurse he thought they were dead. The nurse led John to another operating room. "Do you need something for pain?" It may be a while before your surgery. All the doctors are in surgery with the two trauma patients."

The nurse had mistaken John's tears of joy as tears of pain. "I don't need no medicine woman just tell me what happened?" The nurse could see that he was not going to calm down unless she told him about the talk of the hospital. "The young man was never pronounced dead. Although he has a gun shot wound to the head and has never gained consciousness, he has a good chance for survival if surgery is successful."

"And what about the woman," John asked in excitement.

"Well the woman I hear is a different story. It has been touch and go since they discovered she was still alive in the ambulance. I can tell you she has the best team of surgeons with her now." John was crying openly now. The nurse finally understood. "They were

friends of yours?" John looked at the nurse with tears in his eyes.
"They are friends of mine."

Verna walked into the hospital. Not knowing why she was there.
She went to the seats in the emergency room and sat down. She
had no idea what she was doing. Only that she was supposed to be
there. She was shocked to see Mama Mae and Sam rushing in
through the emergency room doors. They rushed to the front desk
and were being led to another area. Verna jumped up calling
them. Mama Mae ran and hugged Verna holding on tight. Verna
started crying. "You heard about Joy?"

Mama Mae spoke. "Don't worry child Joy will pull through this
surgery and so will Junior." Verna was confused. "What
surgery?"

"The hospital called. Joy was brought in and is in surgery. Junior
is also in surgery," Mama Mae said.

"They're alive," Verna asked?

"Yeah child," Mama Mae said. They have a room for the family
come with us."

Verna became lightheaded. She fainted on the floor.

When Verna awoke she was laying in a hospital bed in a hospital room. John was sitting up in the bed beside her with his arm wrapped up. Verna jumped up. "Is it true?"

John had a serious look on his face. He was doped up from his surgery.

Sam walked in without Mama Mae. "Junior is in recovery. The surgery was successful. He still has not regained consciousness. The next twenty four hours are vital. The doctors will not know until he regains consciousness if there is any brain damage."

Verna was so happy she could not say anything. John groggily asked about Joy.

"Joy is in recovery. She is in extremely critical condition, but she is alive."

Verna and John both began to cry.

Verna asked Sam, "Where is Mama Mae?"

"She is in the chapel praying for Joy and Junior. I have to tell you that your mother and stepfather are here in the recovery waiting room awaiting word on your brother."

Verna became angry. "What about Joy? Did they ask about Joy?" Verna stood up, but became a little dizzy.

"Where are you going," Sam asked?

"I am going to the waiting area for recovery. I want to be there when Joy comes out."

"I don't know if that is a good idea."

"Why?"

"I was told that your mother and stepfather are in that waiting area."

"I am not going to let them stop me from being with my sister."

"I will go with you."

Verna and Sam entered the waiting area. Stepdaddy was sitting by himself in a corner. Sam noticed a scar on his head, a result of being hit in the head years ago by Sam when he tried to take Joy. Stepdaddy immediately noticed Sam and Verna. "I don't want no trouble, old man. I am just here to see about my son. I am sorry about Joy."

Verna could not take it anymore. Her emotions were everywhere. "Sorry! Sorry! Yes, you are sorry; a sorry excuse for a human being. You are not even human. You are an animal. Wasn't it enough what you did to me?" Verna was yelling. "Wasn't it enough! You promised! You Promised!" Sam tried to calm Verna.

Verna's mother walked in the waiting area.

"Verna," Mama said.

Verna turned to face her mother. She had mixed emotions.

"Mama why?"

Mama spoke. "Verna I know you are angry, but this is not the time. I am here to see about Junior and Joy. The doctors said it's amazing how they are stabilizing."

At the mention of Joy, Verna went off again. "You don't care about Joy and you don't care about me. You let that man rape us." At the mention of the rape, Stepdaddy got up and walked out the room.

Mama continued. "I know what happened and it was wrong. Your Stepfather is nothing but an old washed up drunk now. He is miserable and he is paying the price for all the wrong things he has done."

Verna had no sympathy. "Mama you think that makes up for all the hurt he caused us. The fact that he washes his demons away in a bottle, am I supposed to find comfort in that? And what about you Mama, when are you going to pay the price?" Mama was silent for a moment. "I have paid the price and I am still paying the price. I know I can never make it up, but Verna I am sorry. I know about your incarceration. When those Parole board people came to the house to verify that you were being paroled and this was your permanent residence, I told them yes. I wanted to help you."

Verna laughed a hysterical laugh. "Mama, Mama, Mama, you just don't get it do you? It is too late for your help. You should have helped us then." Verna started yelling again. "It's too late Mama! It's too late!" A nurse came in. She tried to calm Verna. She threatened to have security remove her if she did not calm down. Sam had gone to the chapel to get Mama Mae. Mama Mae walked up to Verna and simply grabbed her hand and led her out. Verna did not resist. She could not disrespect this woman who had helped her sister so much. She knew that if Mama Mae had not helped Joy that she would have had the same life that Verna had or even worst. Mama Mae led Verna down to the chapel and sat her down on the pew. They sat there together in silence. Finally Mama Mae spoke to Verna.

"Verna I know you are hurting and you are angry, but what you did in that waiting room was wrong."

Verna was shocked. She looked at Mama Mae.

Mama Mae was firm. "This is not the time for what you did in there. This is the time for faith and prayer."

Verna hung her head. Her emotions had taken control of her. She began to cry. Mama Mae held her as she had held Joy years ago the first night Joy had came to her.

"I know you are hurting child. But you have got to let go of the past."

Verna spoke through her tears. "I can't forget my past. It keeps coming back to me. Because of my past, John was hurt and Junior and Joy might not make it."

"Shut your mouth," Mama Mae demanded. "Joy and Junior will both make it. God has already told me that. Don't let me hear you speak that again. God protected all of you out there on those streets. I know you believe in God."

"I do believe in God Mama Mae, but how come that happened to us?"

"I tell you this, the enemy comes to steal, kill, and destroy. God was with you and it is only because of his presence that John, Junior and Joy are alive right now. Joy and Junior will not die because God has a plan for them and he has a plan for you, but he can not use you right now because you are holding on to your past."

"Mama Mae, how do I let go?"

"Child, you have to forgive."

"I can't."

"Yes you can. Do you think you are the only person who has been hurt? That does not make it right and it sure does not change it, but the past has to stay there. That ugly past is death and as long as you choose to live in it you will be dead. God is life and to choose life you have to first forgive. How can you expect God to forgive you if you can't forgive those who hurt you? Let it go. God will deal with those persons who hurt you. If they do not ask for forgiveness and change their ways, they will have to face the consequences. Now, do you want to let that mess go and live?"

"Yes."

"I want you to pray a special prayer with me." Mama Mae pulled out her old worn Bible. She turned to Psalm 23. She handed Verna the Bible. "Let's pray this prayer together."

"The Lord is my Shepherd; I shall not want. He maketh me to lie down in green pastures: He leadeth me beside the still waters. He restoreth my soul: He leadeth me in the paths of righteousness for his name's sake. Yea, though I walk through the valley of the shadow of death, I will fear no evil: for thou art with me; thy rod and thy staff they comfort me. Thou preparest a table before me in the presence of mine enemies: thou anointest my head with oil; my cup runneth over. Surely goodness and mercy shall follow me all the days of my life: and I will dwell in the house of the Lord for ever. Amen." Verna felt as if a ton of bricks had been lifted off of her. She felt an overwhelming peace. For the first time, she knew that Joy and Junior would survive. "Thank you Mama Mae."

Mama Mae squeezed Verna's hand. "Child, don't thank me, thank God. Now I want you to say that prayer before you and Joy and Junior and John go back out on the streets, every single time. I say this because I know you will go back on the streets again together."

Verna was actually smiling. She believed Mama Mae. "Mama Mae can you show me one more thing?"

"Sure honey."

"Can you show me that scripture about joy coming in the morning?"

"Sure honey, that scripture is also in the book of Psalms. Flip over to Psalms 30 verse 5. Now you read that out loud."

Verna read out loud. "For his anger endureth but a moment; in his favour is life: weeping may endure for a night, but joy cometh in the morning."

Verna felt so relieved. "I can forgive Mama Mae. My joy is coming."

Sam walked in the chapel. He was obviously happy. "Joy and Junior are both out of recovery and are doing very well. Both have been moved to the intensive care unit. The doctors say they will make it."

"I already knew that," Verna said smiling at Mama Mae.

Junior and Joy both continued to miraculously heal. Junior was moved out of intensive care a week later. He had regained consciousness and there did not appear to be any brain damage. He did not remember the incident. Joy was moved out of intensive care six days after Junior. Verna would spend her days and nights visiting both Joy and Junior. There were times that she would cross paths with her mother and Stepdaddy. She did not say anything to them. She knew she had to forgive them, but she could not accept them in her life. Her mother would sometimes bring Joy a gift or two, but she never stayed long. Although Joy was pleasant to their mother, it was obvious that their mother was no longer a part of their lives. Her visits became less and less frequent and the visits eventually stopped. Precious was constantly at the hospital, as well as Renee, who stayed by Junior's side. Finally Junior was released six weeks after the incident. Joy was released nine weeks after the incident fully healed. Mama Mae temporarily moved into the house with Joy and Verna to help take care of Joy, who was still a little weak.

Six months later, Joy met with Junior, John, and Verna. "It is time." Everyone knew what she meant.

The following week, they prepared to go back out to the streets. They all agreed to go back to the area where the incident happened. They felt they had to show the people that they could not be stopped. The work would continue. They caught the train to the well known drug area. After they got off at their stop, Verna stopped everyone. "Before we start there is something we have to do."

She asked everyone to join hands. As she began praying Psalm 23, everyone immediately joined in.

AND GOD SHALL WIPE AWAY ALL

TEARS FROM THEIR EYES: AND THERE

SHALL BE NO MORE DEATH, NEITHER

SORROW, NOR CRYING, NEITHER

SHALL THERE BE ANY MORE PAIN:

FOR THE FORMER THINGS ARE PASSED

AWAY.

REVELATION 21:4

ABOUT THE AUTHOR

Tammy Archibald is a resident of Atlanta, Georgia. She has one daughter, Jasmine. She has a Bachelor's Degree in Sociology and Criminal Justice from Old Dominion University in Norfolk, Virginia. She has worked for the Department of Corrections and currently works as a Juvenile Court Probation Officer.

Printed in the United States
24301LVS00001B/25-30